Ma Wee Stc

PB

Cher Bonfis

Ma Wee Stories

Cher Bonfis: - Born in a 'Long House' belonging to Iban people on the Island of Borneo. That very night an Orang-utan swooped in from the jungle thicket and stole the newborn baby raising the child as her own. Thirteen years went by before the now teenage Cher was discovered and returned to Scotland where she was immediately confined to a hospital bed having become 'chilled' by the contrast of the heat of the Borneo jungle and Buchanan Street, Glasgow. Sorry that was a lie… Is it worth beginning again? Probably not, for the words written here, or in some newspaper, would not really allow you to access the mind of this author. If you want to know about this person best you read the things this person writes. Trivia over details of this life are irrelevant. What you should know is that there is much gratitude for your interest and there is hope that you have found something rewarding. If you believe in love and kindness. If you believe everyone deserves a chance to live a happy life then you and Cher Bonfis have a lot in common. Word by word we will strive to make things better. So thank you for stopping by, and may all good things be yours.

Ma Wee Stories

Cher Bonfis

Lulach Publishing

Copyright © Cher Bonfis and Lulach Publications 2024

The right of Cher Bonfis to be identified as author of this work has been asserted in accordance with the Copyright, Designs and Patents Act 1988. All characters and events described in this book are fictional and any resemblance to actual persons, living or dead, is purely coincidental.

Published by Lulach Publishing 2024

https://www.lulachpublishing.com

All rights reserved. Except for the quotation of short passages for the purposes of criticism and review, no part of this publication may be reproduced, stored in a retrieval system, or transmitted, in any form or by any means, electronic, mechanical, photocopying, recording or otherwise, without the prior permission of the publisher.

Cher Bonfis
Ma Wee Stories

British Library cataloguing in Publication Data. A Catalogue record for this book is available from the British Library.

ISBN 978-1-7396723-4-8
BIC categories:- FA,

Typeset in Elatan

PB

*These stories are works of fiction.
Some public figures are mentioned.
Any other names or characters,
businesses or places,
events or incidents, are fictitious.
Any resemblance to actual persons,
living or dead, is purely coincidental.*

Reading for six minutes each day can, they say, reduce stress by 68% and they also say it can help people read more fluently and many feel it is the ultimately the most relaxing of pastimes. (all those except for those who go fishing of course)

Scottish Libraries started 'Keep the heid and read!' and people pledge to read six minutes per day. https://keeptheheid.scot/

So this book contains many short stories which, depending on how quickly you read, may well help with that.

Sighted people learn 83% of all they know through their eyes and reading seems to enter your brain in a more 'solid' form than other media.

Oh I have no idea who they are.

Ma Wee Stories

Page	Story Title	Number
20	Red Shoes	1
21	It Matters Rose	2
22	City in the Sun	3
23	Out of the Snow	4
24	Bread Butter and Jam	5
25	The Wedding is Off	6
26	Anything is Possible	7
27	Barcelona	8
28	Listening	9
29	Perchance to Dream	10
30	Old Car	11
31	Single Bed	12
32	Frog Horse and Lion	13
33	An Open Fire	14
34	A Tree	15
35	Blowing Hot and Cold	16
36	Marie Kelly and Sonja	17
37	The View	18
38	One Hundred	19
39	Advertising	20
40	Whisky Fire Light	21
41	Who Are You?	22
42	Wheat	23
43	Passport	24
44	Gossip	25
45	Butterflies	26
46	High Pressure	27
47	Olongapo	28

	14 Cher Bonfis	
48	Answer the Phone	29
49	Kiss	30
50	My Men	31
51	The Good Old Days	32
52	The Age Gap	33
53	I Loved Acting	34
54	Romeo	35
55	Ruby Red	36
56	Risk	37
57	Travelling Light	38
58	Blood	39
59	Accident	40
60	Lilacs	41
61	Declamation	42
62	I Had to Say	43
64	The Singer	44
66	The AA Box	45
68	Barbie	46
70	A Breathe of Air	47
72	Loon and the Moon	48
74	Use Your Vote	49
76	Changi	50
78	Miss You	51
80	For Sale	52
82	Expensive Education	53
84	Hedgehog	54
86	Come Back	55
88	Fortune	56
90	Taste	57
92	Bramley	58

	Ma Wee Stories	15
94	Nineteen Years	59
96	Holiday for Everyone	60
98	Sparrow	61
100	Reality	62
102	Bye Bye	63
104	Garbage	64
106	Too Hot	65
108	The Horse that Passed Wind	66
110	Sleeping in the Car	67
112	Politics	68
114	Roast Tatties	69
116	Independent	70
118	Midnight Swim	71
120	White Bread Rolls	72
122	Soft White Rolls	73
124	Telegrams	74
126	Away to the Hills	75
128	Who Would Have Thought?	76
130	I Do	77
132	Regulate	78
134	Ice Cream	79
136	The News	80
138	The Children	81
140	Time	82
142	House in the Country	83
144	The Shock	84
146	Enlighten	85
148	Leonard Cohen	86
150	Independence	87
152	John	88

16	Cher Bonfis	
154	Rich and Poor	89
156	The Last Note	90
158	Turning Back the Clock	91
160	Divorce	92
162	Divorce from the Other Side	93
164	Imagination	94
166	Old Friends	95
168	It Comes to Us All	96
170	Algorithms	97
172	A Fabulous Evening	98
174	The Coat Hanger	99
176	Spot Light	100
178	Breathe it in	101
180	Procrastination	102
182	Mackerel	103
184	Lists	104
186	Insurance	105
188	Nurture and Culture	106
190	Nothing	107
192	Borneo	108
194	The Entertainer	109
196	Climate Control	110
198	I've Lost Scot	111
200	To Enjoy Later	112
202	Sounds Like a Week	113
204	High Pressure Barometer	114
206	Felled Like a Sitka Spruce	115
208	New Knees	116
210	The Shortest Day	117
212	Bonnie Wee Queanee	118

	Ma Wee Stories	17	
214	A Photograph with Jimmy	119	
216	Something and Nothing	120	
218	Home to Aberdeen	121	
220	Has Love Been Good to You?	122	
222	A Tribe	123	
224	Jimmy	124	
226	I Wish You Still Could	125	
228	It Sounds as if Something is Broken	126	
230	Numbers	127	
232	The Three Musketeers	128	
234	Last March	129	
236	Glass Bottom Boat	130	
238	All the Way to Berlin	131	
240	If Only	132	
242	Disappointments	133	
244	Limping	134	
246	Bryony	135	
248	25 Years of Blanket	136	
250	Washing Machines	137	
252	The Singalong	138	
254	The Key Ring	139	
256	The Book Stop	140	
258	Cloud Burst Situation	141	
261	Staying Awake	142	
264	New Hip	143	
267	The Machine that goes Ping	144	
270	Justice?	145	
273	Cnut	146	
276	Carpet	147	

279	Donna Music Queen	148
283	Empathy	149
287	Harmony	150
291	Leave	151
295	King Charles III	152
299	Dalrymple	153
303	Handyman	154
308	Goldfish	155
327	Thawing Snow	156
328	Just in Case	157

Ma Wee Stories

Red Shoes

Diana loved those red shoes it took so long to save the money to buy them. She rushed from work and managed to get to the shop before it closed. There was only one pair left and she was in luck they were in her size. She paid and then clutched the bag in her hand and headed for the train station. Diana was singing that song *Walking on Sunshine* in her head as she opened her front door. It was not a palace, she lived alone and she was lonely. She put the bag down on her table and then she showered. The bag sat there and she was imagining she was the *Christmas girl*, that her sweet daddy had so cherished so many years ago. She remembered the presents beneath the tree and all the excitement of having to wait until Christmas day to open them. It was not Christmas now it was July and today Diana was twenty-five years old, no one else in the world knew that it was her birthday. She prepared her evening meal, she washed up the dishes and cleaned her kitchenette. Then she put on the red dress she had given herself last year and she carefully unwrapped this year's gift. She eased them on to her feet and stood looking at herself in the full-length mirror. She smiled and said out loud 'Happy Birthday' Diana.

It Matters Rose

Thanking me for support in these strange times. It is interesting to me, as I have only just begun to be involved in the *Social Media Revolution* and suddenly I am in deep conversation via the chat feature with someone far away in another land that I have never seen face to face. Extraordinary! These are strange times indeed. The worldwide pandemic has changed us all and we will not be the same after it has been controlled. I have changed already. For a whole year I have been at home, only the occasional trip out to get groceries. Most of my life I have hurtled about with hardly a moment to breathe. Having had a lot of time to breathe I have heard bits of my body squeal for attention. The pains in my legs after driving I used to ignore now they will not keep quiet. I suspect they are not so happy with the extra weight, no matter how many walks or goes on my rebounder I have not managed to keep trim. The bit between my ears has also been troubled it has been a fight to keep the difference between sanity and insanity. What has astonished me has been the support that has come my way from friends and also those from the people I have not met except on *Social Media* I have never physically met these people but such kindness from people I have never met is inspiring. So I am in a position now when I must thank each and everyone who has supported me during this strange time and for all the years I have been alive. I know I am a lucky one, I know not everyone has received what I have, so thank you for reading this for that too is support. Lets go on supporting and caring. Good wishes and luck to you.

City in the Sun

Back then, when it was easy, one could travel out of *Lavington* to the north passing the armed guards in their dark blue *Securicor Ford Transit* vans. Out of the 'high income suburb' and join the A104 turn left heading west. I suppose you could say heading for the heart of the 'dark continent'. Yes I heard people call it that even in the 1980s. The road follows out past *Kinoo* and *Kikuyu* and heads to the north. Then just before you get to *Limuru* you need to make a left folk onto the B3 and in a while you were there. It must have been one hundred kilometres. You could go on into the town but if you want to see the lake best turn left after *Karagita*. Back then there were flocks of flamingos glowing pink in the sun, sometimes they would take to the sky and circle then splash back down again. Some folk used to take boats out on the water. There were hippopotamus you would not want to disturb one of them and make it upset but they were my favourites. The pelicans with their fabulous beaks so wonderful. Back then there were African villages where the houses were made from the brown-red mud with reed roofs. You could see the women in their colourful clothes cooking on Jiko stoves.

Out of the Snow

The alpine snow glistened in the cold January sun. The tall black man came from the glow and the snow in a contrast that was seen or missed. He obviously had some notion of me for he chose to speak English and not in Swiss German. His words hang with me today and they still make me smile. "Hello I am from Nigeria, and I am looking for some space to store some things"!!!! What? You know how fear blocks off the thoughts and focuses on how you can escape? Well I had no idea who this man was, but I had certainly read that 'round robin' email about someone having *squillions* of US dollars which they had to look after for the 'Nigerian Oil Corporation' and if I would just put it in my bank account for a few days, I could enjoy an enormous reward! I took a deep breath and said "Well you are a new person to me and I know nothing of you so I think that before I head down the route of storing things for you we would need to get to know one another better. After all until you get to know me how do you know your things would be safe?" Time went by and he showed up once in a while and before long I did make room for his 'stuff'. He had worked out that Swiss people often want the latest version of a product and although the pervious version still had a deal of life in it they would throw the old away. So he collected the 'chuck outs' and transported them to Nigeria, where he sold the stuff he made money for his family and for a charity he started to care for orphaned children. We became friends.

Bread Butter and Jam

The butter was creamy, the bread was soft, the jam was sweet and fruity. The orange juice had been freshly squeezed. Timothy sat down on a chair by the table in his garden. The sun was shining and there was a coolness in the breeze. Throughout his life he had wrestled with that 'drive' that made him work and work and work. Always must he be doing something. So he had, everyday, to work. Always there for his children. At the beck and call of his wife. Always time for a wee job his neighbour needed doing. Sometimes he thought that time was like the elastic in the band of his trousers always a bit more stretch for a wee pancake or a *yum yum*. However had he done it all? Now here he was the children grown the wife flown, living in the countryside away from neighbours and all their 'would you have a moment?' 'It won't take long'. Here was Timothy retired into a heavenly landscape. He made his own bread and he squeezed the oranges he bought in the village the day before. The jam was from the strawberries he had grown last summer. He sat down in the sun but he was still trying to keep his brain in control trying to stop it from looking for the next job that was of course so vital that it could not wait. He looked around the garden all was in order. He had painted the outside of the house, it was gleaming white in the sun. There was nothing more that had to have his attention. What next? He asked himself. He picked up the glass of orange juice. Then he ate the bread with the butter and jam.

The Wedding is Off

"There will not be a wedding. That's the big news." "Why?" "I just decided it would be better not too. We are so different." "Is that not the point? Opposites attract." "Yes I know and from that perspective we really are poles apart. I don't know, I just want to get up and do things. If I want him to do things with me I have to chase. Oh he is happy to tag along but oh I want more." "He has been really good to you. Is he not upset?" "No everything is good and since we decided not to get married things are so much easier." "So where are you living?" "We are still in the apartment but I am moving out, we are going to look at apartments at the weekend." "We?" "Yes he is helping me, he is being very good about it!" "Oh, he is? I see."

.

I really did not know what to say. I just did not believe that he was happy about it. A few weeks ago they were going to buy a flat. Still they are young. I just thought…...What will happen to their cats?

Anything is Possible

He gave me a box of chocolates he whispered in my ear that it was a token of his love. I smiled and felt so warm inside they were my favourites. I had only closed my eyes for a moment but when I opened them I found that he was kneeling on one knee. Then he said the words to the question I had wanted to hear for so long. The cynics will say that I am an old softie that I am all tied up in romance. To them I say I do not have a problem with that. The man to whom I am now engaged is the finest of our species he is good, kind, strong and brave and he will marry me next summer. My best friend will be my bridesmaid we have known each other since our first day in school. I will be wearing the same white dress that my mother wore when she was married to my dear old dad. It has been a long road but when Simon told me he wanted me to be his girl he said he would ask me to marry him as soon as he could afford to buy us a proper house to live in. We fell in love in nineteen-eighty and now we are both fifty-seven years old. Neither of us wanted to have a family of our own. All these years we have rented our separate apartments two streets from each other and finally after forty-two years he has honoured his promise and so we will live under our own roof. We saved and we paid for this house it is ours. I live in hope that we will rest long beneath it's ceilings and be healthy. If we live here for forty-two years we will both be ninety-nine years old by then provided dementia and illness give us a by we might even make one-hundred. Anything is possible.

Barcelona

"For goodness sake the police in Barcelona are not going to worry about a seventy five year old Scotsman waving a Saltire and suggesting to the locals that I support their bid to be independent from Madrid in the same way I want Scotland to be independent of London." "Well maybe the difference is that the politician's of the 'Cortes Generals' (The Spanish Parliament), in Madrid, can get really upset when Catalonia raises it's voice in favour of breaking away from Spain. Those in Madrid say that The Spanish Constitution says that Spain is an 'indissoluble unity'." "Well they are entitled to their opinion, but so am I." "When you are home in Scotland sure, but in Barcelona you will be a foreign tourist." "So that stops me from having my voice heard does it? What will they do arrest me?" "Well you never know. You must have heard of the 'Rapper' who was sent to prison for nine months because they said he slandered the Spanish crown and the Institutions of the State, they also said he was glorifying terrorism. The rapper says he has a right to free speech. Well there was a demonstration to protest about this. In that crowd was a young Scotsman he was lifted from the street by police and he has been in prison for a couple of weeks already without being sent for trail. Remember too they sent nine Catalonian politicians to prison for holding a referendum. No I think strongly that you would be well advised not to take your Saltire on holiday with you." "You know what you have just made me want to pack several."

Listening

He saw it on a TV show. They put a glass on a wall then leaned their ear in against the glass so the glass would not fall from the wall. The idea was that you could hear conversations that were going on in the room the other side of the wall the glass was held against. To Graham's astonishment it actually worked. As soon as he had positioned the glass and his ear he could clearly hear what was being said. There were two voices a man and a woman. The man said, "Well it's too late now, you really should have thought of that before." She replied. "Oh that's right never take the blame yourself. It always has to be my fault." He then said, "Well if the cap fits wear it." The women shrieked a piercing scream. There was a loud bang, like the sound of a gun being fired in a TV cop show. Graham continued to listen. He thought he could hear the scraping of a chair across a wooden floor. He thought he heard the sound of a door opening and a little later a door closing. Graham stood back in the shadow of his room and peered out of the window, to the front yard, of his neighbour's house. He saw his neighbour heaving something in the back of his old estate car.

Perchance to Dream

I was in Germany on a tour. My cousin was in the British Army. I went to his barracks and he said that I was welcome to sleep the night in a room in the 'Sergeants Mess'. Six o'clock, the following morning, he loudly entered the room, in camouflage battle dress, holding a huge gun in his arms, whilst screaming at the top of his voice! I have no idea why he did that. He frightened me ridged. Never have I engaged with him in anyway since without recalling the terror of the way he jolted me from my dreams that bright sunny morning on the Lüenburger Heide.

It was an all night party; I was sixteen years of age. We stayed awake until about five, by that time there was a mixture of sleeping bodies, and half awake bodies, scattered about the room. I was cold; I dozed for an hour or two, Then people started shifting and shuffling about, until there was no choice but to join them and sleepwalked all the way home. Where I promptly fell into bed and slept most of the day. Until I heard my mothers voice asking where the hell I had been all the previous night.

Old Car

My old car would not restart. I just needed a rest the journey was long. A few minutes rest with my eyes closed. Then there was simply no life in the battery. The lay-by was dark and lonesome it was summer but it was cold. My jacket was too thin but dozed off again. For how long I am not sure. I awoke to a banging on the glass by my right ear. A torch beam shone into my eyes. I caught the glimpse of a police car. The policeman was investigating he wondered if I was OK. Well I was before he had arrived. I asked for a push. He said no. I was cross. Maybe some static electricity in me charged the battery when I pressed the start button in my anger and the engine roared into life and I headed on my journey. At school they made us say a prayer 'if I die before I wake I pray my lord my soul you take.' So just to let you know I was lucky enough to wake up again today, I think that is amazing.

Single Bed

At the time I cannot tell you just how much he had annoyed me. Every morning without fail he would look into my eyes and tell me how much he loved me. He said he would always love me for I gave him his wonderful children; he said he would always love me for that. I wonder if he still does? All these mornings now I awake on my own, I should change this double bed for a single and then maybe I would feel less alone. I have only myself to blame of course, I know it is true. That great man I harmed him. They told me how lucky I was to find him after our first date. He was always there he did all that had to be done. He provided more than anyone had the right to expect. Our children had horses, I had lovely clothes and always a beautiful car. Nothing to be done about that now. It was just something primeval inside me. I just wanted to try something else. The man I chose was not good looking, he was rough and he spoke coarsely. I took a chance I just had too. What were the chances that anyone would find out? What if they did? Was it such a big drama? Not at the time but when I was caught out then it was and it still is. I am still in the house my wonderful husband diligently made for us. I still have the bed but wish now that I still had the man who bought it. I wish he would look in my eyes and tell me once more how he loves me.

Frog Horse and Lion

Once upon a giant metal horse was a bright green frog. When I say this frog was bright green I really mean bright. He was bright in colour and in mind. He said "Mind you Mr. Horse I was once in Africa, there deep in a green forest I watched a very special lion. He could not see me because I am green and the forest was green so I melted into the background of the forest canopy, camouflaged." Then the metal horse spoke. "Well tell me what you saw my little green companion." The green frog said. "No I have a much better idea let us go there right now and you can see for yourself. It is always better to see for yourself." So the metal horse and it's rider, the bright green frog, set off upon their long journey. They turned right at the end of the street then the mystical metal horse launched himself into the sky, they flew through the blue and in and out of the clouds. They travelled for six weeks, two days and three hours and forty-five seconds. Then they were there, the bright green frog melted into the green of the forest. The lion awoke from his afternoon sleep he looked up and said: "What are you doing here?"

An Open Fire

They certainly were not rich but the pit provided a home, food and coal which kept a family well. Until prime minister *Thatcher* closed it all down. Most of the houses in the mining village were pulled down as families left to find their livings elsewhere in other work. The community which had supported them all throughout the long cold miners strike of 1984-1985. *Thatcher* verses *Arthur Scargill* with troops of striking miners pitted against an army of policemen. Shields and batons the police were bussed in from all over into a mining culture that was previously unknown to them. To control and bring the coal miners to heel *Ian MacGregor,* the industrialist and manager of the National Coal Board, had already had a good crack at curbing the steel industry. He started on the coal in 1983. One of the benefits of being a miner was a good supply of coal to burn in the hearth of the open fire in the living room of the tiny dwellings in which big families grew. The fire has gone out in the few miners cottages that remain. Some of the folk who were born here still remain but they grow older, soon they will be no more. So new people arrive and they take up the cottages but with no coal to burn the fireplaces are covered and hidden in the wall.

A Tree

I planted a Silver Birch tree today. I have always been attracted by the colour of the bark of the Silver Birch. It is a pretty little thing, when I say little it is already taller than me. When I started to dig the hole for it the sun was still in the southwest behind the house. The leaves had a deep green about them. Now as I look from my window to the garden the sun is in the northeast and it's rays are flowing through the branches and leaves of this new tree. The leaves are light green and sparkling. So I wish this tree long life. I hope that many people, insects, birds and animals will profit from it's presence. Now it is a young sapling, it should be here a long time after I am gone. It could still be here in 2121. If it is and global warming has flooded the lower grounds around here maybe it will be on an island like a cartoon desert island with a palm tree. I hope that this little tree will grow tall it could grow to thirty meters, maybe it helps a little in the fight to save us from climate catastrophe. Apparently the people from Finland beat themselves with Silver Birch branches whilst bathing during sessions in the sauna. The wood can be used to make furniture, parquet flooring and it is very easy to burn. The bark contains a resin which is very useful some people even make shoes from strips of birch bark. The one I planted is *Betula Pendula Alba P CR* I picked it out because of the *ALBA* (pronounced AL AH BA) Alba is Scottish Gaelic for Scotland and was often used to refer to the part of Scotland north of the *Firth of Forth*. It has been a happy day the sun is setting through the leaves now. Saor Alba - Alba gu bràth Scotland Forever. We often call these trees Birks.

Blowing Hot and Cold

Mid May slightly closer to June it feels no warmer than it has for months. I think there might be a frost again tonight. My poor plants look up at me from my garden I am sure if they could speak they would complain that life is far to cold for them here. I have waited so many years I have waited for climate change to warm the north where I come from, now I see that climate change is far from warming for my homeland. Instead the arctic ice is melting cold water is flooding the oceans and it is pushing the warming *Gulf Stream* south. Every night in April we had frost. I read that the melting ice has shifted the axis of the globe. It seems that some people have started changing their habits, their diets, the way they transport themselves from here to there. Years ago I planted two thousand six hundred and two trees they are mature now. If I can save another four thousand pounds I can buy a piece of land and then I could plant some more. The oceans are flooding paradise islands, glaciers have disappeared, some summers are too hot, there are some places that should always be cold but they are warming and the permafrost is melting. Minnesota zoo have killed two elderly Musk Ox, They were old and were suffering their age the spring and summer heat are were too much for them. We keep producing, consuming, throwing our rubbish here there and everywhere. What are the chances of that stopping? Slim I think. Will we evolve so quickly that we can deal with the new environment we are creating? Will we become extinct?

PB

Marie Kelly and Sonja

Since we left school the girls and I meet twice a year for a 'Girls Night Out'. We started at primary then moved to the Secondary Modern then we all went to the Further Education College and did City and Guilds in hairdressing. We all qualified and we have all be able to make our own businesses. It is like having two of the best sisters any girl could ever have. We have been bridesmaids for each other and we each have husband and a boy and a girl each. All I can say is that we all feel as if we have lived charmed lives, what are the chances of us all reaching forty in the absence of major trauma? That changed yesterday, Tom, Marie's husband was in an accident his car was hit by a truck. He went off to work as normal seven o'clock sharp. He was going to do a job fifteen miles from here. It was a fine sunshine full morning, that is what probably caused the accident. The police said that they thought the truck driver was blinded by the light and did not see Tom's car. Marie, Kelly and I are waiting in the hospital now. Tony and Dave are looking after the kids. Excuse me that is my mobile I must take this: "Hello. Yes love. No we don't know yet. Yes we are waiting. He is in a very bad way. I really don't know. Listen I will call you when we have some news." "Sonja, quick." Called Marie. "What has happened?"

The View

If you walk up the brae from here then just before the gate which leads into the farm, take the wee path that follows the dry stonewall and head on for the hills. You will see the cairn long before you reach it, remember to add your stone to the pile. You will see a large bolder by the cairn. Scramble up on to it and take in the view, it matters not which way you choose to look you will see heaven in all directions. Swivel your body around through three hundred and sixty degrees; see which you think is the most spectacular. Remember every view looks different depending upon the time of day you look and of course the weather. Towards the south you will be caught up in the heather and sheep, the lambs will be quite big this late in the season. The hill looks wild, barren but the different shades of dark and light green contrast with the white fleeces of the sheep, who will stare back at you as if they really cared. To the left of your vision is the seam between the hills you were just looking at and a rock face with jagged edges. Deep dark greys and blacks punctuated by the odd bit of gorse clinging to the side of the stack of rocks. I am only outlining the basics here. Looking to the northeast there is a forest of great tall trees dark green pine, the forest stretches on and on, and on. To the northwest is the small loch and if you are lucky there could be Canada-geese with their babies, so beautiful. I have told you enough, it is time to go and look for yourself.

One Hundred

"I am sorry Sir, your card has been declined." "Yes well I am not surprised there has been no money coming in for about six months." "Am I to understand Sir, that you came in to this restaurant you ordered a meal for yourself and this lady in full knowledge that you had no funds to pay for your dinner?" "That is not quite right I thought that there might be enough, it seems that there wasn't." "Well what do you propose to do about settling your bill, Sir? You have eaten three courses, including T bone steak and a bottle of fine Champaign." "The meal was delicious, the steak was cooked to perfection, the Champaign one of the most superb I have ever drunk, and I can tell you I have drunk a few, on my travels around the world. I am not really sure what I can do about payment, just at this time. I am sure things will look up sometime soon." "Well, Sir, I am afraid that this is not the way I can run my business, if customers eat my finest fare and then cannot fund the bill at the end of the evening, it is simply not a sustainable business model." "Do you have washing up that requires doing?" "Please, Sir, do not make ridiculous suggestions." "So it is no good offering to make instalment payments?" "Sir!" "Hey it is OK I was just winding you up that card I gave you is an old one, you should have checked the expiry date. Use this card and add one hundred to the bill as my tip."

Advertising

Think about it…. They have enough resources to advertise on the television. Why would they do that? They say all the things to make you think they are doing this or that to benefit you. They tell you that you are the one who will gain; you are the one who will benefit. They tell you how good it will be for you and how little it will cost you, how long it will last, how it will make you more attractive, how it will improve your standing in the world. You can buy it now no deposit, minimum payments, which will not begin for five years….. FIVE YEARS! By that time the kids will have drawn all over it with magic marker, it will have coffee and wine stains which you will cover with a throw. All those years to become 'mortgage free' and now you are free of mortgage and children the best thing you can do, so 'they' tell you, is to take advantage of the increased value of your house and release the equity. Spend your twilight years rolling in the luxury of loads of cash, then when you are dead we will own your house and it will make no difference to you, you will no longer need it. It will affect your children and what they inherit from you. They will charge fees at the front of the deal. We are thinking of the environment, making sure you are safe, protected, and we source all our materials responsibly. Why not be a vegan? Colour your hair with this. No hair use this. Make-up use this because everyone is worth it. Well we are all sales persons really, whatever it is we have to offer.

Whisky Fire Light

Many people love the aroma they long for cold days when they can sit close and watch the red glow as it smoulders. Even on summer evenings the chill can easily fall in the north. It takes thousands of years to grow and although it burns slowly it does not take more than moments to disappear as smoke through the lum (chimney). There are many words to describe it for over the years it has been used in many places by many people. When I was a wean we called it *the moss*, many call it peat. Sadly I never found the scent easy it always climbed into my lungs in a disagreeable way. I preferred burning the whisky barrels. The barrels or casks are made from oak in the cooperage. The Cooper, an ancient professional crafts person, send the barrels to Spain where the sherry makers use them for many years making their fortified wine. When they have done with the barrels they return them to Scotland to the makers of 'The Water of Life' – Whisky. The distillers create their amber nectar from malted barley and fine spring water. They then seal it away in the barrels and a wee bit of that Sherry mingles with the new whisky as it matures for many, many years. Once the whisky has been decanted into bottles the barrel is of no more use to the distillers. So some companies buy them and turn them into furniture. Tables, chairs, boxes to store blankets. Any off cuts are sold off as firewood. They delivered them off a pick-up truck and the smell was wonderful. Oh how they burned so warm and bright. Whisky fire light.

Who Are You?

"You say you don't know who I am. Well I, I am standing here and until a moment ago I had no idea of who you are. If the truth be known I really have no idea who you are really. My question is this. Why would I want to be someone other than who I am? Don't you think I have enough trouble being me without trying to be someone else too? I mean really, I have a job getting through the day as it is being little old me. How many mornings have I woken up thinking 'will I be able to navigate this old hulk of a body to yet another sunset?' Or should I pack me up and become someone else for the day? So is this *pass* enough to prove to you that I am me? How do I know that 'Identity Card' you waved at me is real? I have never seen a specimen sample. I have no idea what a real ID card of someone that you are claiming to be would look like. So I ask myself is this person really who they say they are and appear to be? I mean I know what I just said but isn't everybody someone else sometimes? Come on when you are singing in the shower you maybe washing you body but in your head, come on be honest now, you are really thinking 'I am *Elvis*.... 'Since my baby left me I found an new place to dwell, no go on it's ok, down at the end of lonely street at heartbreak hotel.' I always fancied myself as a *Roger Daltrey*. What do you mean I don't look a bit like him? That is hardly the point I have been trying to make. Look I don't know who you are but I am telling you I am me. The question really is *WHO ARE YOU?*"

Wheat

For countless years I have puzzled over a question. I have asked it many times of many people and I do not think any of them really listened to what I wanted them to answer. Here is the question….when confronted with a sea of grasses, how on earth did our ancestors find the grass we now call wheat?

Further how did they workout that that was the one that was good to eat. Further how on earth did they workout how to add yeast water and salt to make bread?

Passport

It was his seventy-fifth birthday. People had stopped blowing out candles on cakes back in the 2020/21 Covid Pandemic. Vaughan was not a great lover of cake anyway. It was a nice party, he was amazed that so many people had shown up to celebrate. It was 2031. Life was tough, the problems with climate change, and more and more people. It was a tradition in his family that a speech was made by the birthday person. The tradition ran that the speech was to highlight important positive moments. Vaughan began. "Ten years ago, I lived in hope that one day our beautiful country would become free and Independent. I had never thought it was given, I always felt we had to work hard to convince everyone that it was the right thing for us all. Imagine, if you can, well of course you can, you were all with me that night when they raised the Saltire. I thought that was probably the most positive moment, of my life, apart from marriage and the children. Although it was top of my list of my best days I felt even better the day my *Scottish Passport* arrived. Oh but then there was an even better day the day, the sweet day, I went on holiday. I arrived in Barcelona aboard a hydrogen-fuelled plane. I held out my beautiful new passport for the Catalonian border police. I can tell you my heart could have bounced out of my chest. However, that was not the biggest moment that came at the end of my holiday. The plane landed in Edinburgh and I presented that passport to our border police. Now it is my ambition to live long, and happy, and to use it again and again."

Gossip

"Did you see him last night?" "Yes, but not for long, he was in a hurry." "Him? In a Hurray? Are you sure? I can hardly believe that." "Yes well he has that reputation, everyone thinks he is lazy." "Lazy! You are the darling of the understatement." "He did tell me what he has been doing these past two months." "Doing?" "Yes. I think we may have got him all wrong." "So what has he been up to? Come on spill the beans." "I can't. I promised him I would not tell anyone." "What! Don't be stupid you can tell me. I wouldn't say a word." "Well actually he specifically asked me not to tell you in particular." "What? Who the heck does he think he is? Suggesting I cannot keep a secret." "Well he said that you do most of the gossiping around here." "Oh he did, did he? What about you? It seems to me you can tell a tale or two." "Oh I see turning the tables are you?" "No. I was just saying." "What did you say to Kirsty about me? Walls have ears you should know that." "I didn't say anything." "Well Paula told me you did. I can't help the way I have put on weight." "Well I did say it was after your last pregnancy." "Well what right did you think you have to talk about me behind my back?" "Anyway Martha told me that you said my new hair style makes me look older!" "Well it does!" "Well you have put on weight. You should not wear those blue jeans anymore." "Well you should get your hair re-coloured as soon as you can." "Oh don't go into a sulk. Every time we have a little discussion." "I'm not sulking. I don't sulk." "Oh go on tell me what he has been doing." "Oh alright, but you must promise never to tell another soul."

Butterflies

My new neighbours have a wee loon (boy) not yet two years. He is bright as an LED torch and has a smile which could put the sun in shade. The first time he came into my kitchen with his mum he became transfixed by the ceiling. On it there are dozens of plastic butterflies. Many sizes, many different colours. The ceiling has delighted many people since I created it six years ago. The butterflies are scattered in random fashion often the glue pads which fix them in the air fail and they flutter to the floor it makes them sort of real when they fly about like that. At the end of August if we get a few hot sunny days the Buddleia and the Privet in the garden are very attractive to real life live butterflies Painted Lady, Red Admiral, Tortoise Shell, Peacock and the occasional Cabbage White. The wee loon was fascinated by them. So I ordered a new set of these plastic butterflies. I said to his dad that he and his boy can stick some on my kitchen ceiling and then take the rest and put them somewhere in their house. I will let you know how that goes.

High Pressure

How many weather people are there? Every time you watch the telly there is another. Switch on the radio and yet more. Where do they all come from? I suppose you have to be ambitious to become a weather person who appears on screen. Do broadcasters advertise for them? Is there a special school where they all go to learn how to do it? How do they do it? All those pictures, all that information, all in such a short space of time. Then the cheery 'Farewell…. 'Enjoy your evening.' Just after the announcement of a summer storm with gale force winds. Who remembers what they say the next day, when they are standing in a pool of sunshine, thinking the prediction was for rain? Well no one gets everything right all the time. Really does anyone really care? After all you can do nothing but accept what happens anyway! What would we be without them and what would broadcasters do to fill the space if there were not weather forecasts. You know if you had listened to weatherman, Sean, he told you to protect your new plants from the frost, you smiled and thought 'oh come on it is May already we don't have frost in May', but we did. So when Charlotte tells you to be careful of the ultraviolet wear the sunscreen and a hat listen to her and do as you are told. When Philip says remember your umbrella take it with you and save yourself from getting wet. Wishing you plenty of high summer pressure and a steady barometer.

Olongapo

On 31 October 1983 I was in a town called Olongapo in the Philippines. I kept a diary of that trip and these past days I have been referring to it as I write some memoirs. As it happens to be 31 October 2021 I have a snippet of the dairy to share with you 31 October 1983 was Halloween and Olongapo was to have a German Oktober Fest. The streets were decorated, and there were carnival floats and everyone was in costume. That was the evening. The dawn had arrived very early with the air-con sounding much like *Terry Wogan* (sorry I was not a fan of the breakfast radio broadcaster) in my ears. To my surprise I had not been molested in the night. I used my 'emergency' bottle of disinfectant and scrubbed out the hotel room shower and lavatory. I washed my stinging sunburn and then went out into the street. It was a street of a million Tricycles—motor bikes with side cars and Jeepneys—converted World War Two jeeps, decorated, extended and now used as a taxi/buses. Everyone of the drivers seemed to want to give me a lift. I wanted to walk, and have a good look at the town. It was a bustling place the shops had a huge verity of stock; they were interspersed by bars, and massage parlours, gay clubs and clinics which, boldly listed all the ailments they could cure. Through the windows of the bars I could see young girls sleeping in chairs, I think it must have been a hard life even with the income that American Servicemen, of The Subic Base, provided.

Answer the Phone

"Oh sorry we were just about to have lunch, could you call back later?" I clicked the button and ended the call. My next thought was 'Why answer the phone if you have not the time for a conversation?' Maybe just habit, maybe the feeling that at last someone might care, maybe they answered realise it was you and thought 'Oh No!', maybe they thought 'Oh what do they want now?' So why did you call them? To see if they were well and healthy. Why did you bother? Do they ever call you to find out if you are well and healthy? No, I cannot remember them ever calling me to see if I was well and healthy. Oh they did call when they needed overnight accommodation because they had a conference to attend. Yes you prepared the room and made them breakfast, yes they did say thank you but you haven't seen them since then and that was several years ago. Will you call back later? If you do not will they call you? There you have it 'could you call back later?' If only the conversation had gone 'Oh I had to answer because I saw it was you but we have folk in for lunch right now. I really want to find out how you are doing. Will it be good if I call back after four this afternoon?

Kiss

I saw a newspaper article from one of those awful papers it read: *men have an average of 7.6 sexual partners whilst women have only 2.6!* Who did the maths on that I wonder? Were these heterosexual or homosexual unions? Did they mean full sex or was fooling about included? Is the average different in different countries or between different races? I have often wondered how actors have the audacity to recite lines like 'the sex was great', 'that sex was better than any'. Fewer than 8 or fewer than 3 partners does not give to much experience to compare or contrast. So I scratched around in my memory I do not know about you but good or bad did not really come into it was more like this 'at last someone will do this with me!' I can remember having sex with seventeen different women, and I fooled about with quite a few more. I cannot tell you, but then I doubt any of them could tell you either, if the sex was earth movingly great. I tell you what I do remember. There was pretty girl I met, she lived in a street not far from my house. There was a chance to ask her out for dinner and she accepted the invitation, we did not have sex nor did we fool around but as we parted she leaned over and kissed me on the lips so lightly and delicately it was as if I had been kissed by silk. Then she was gone. I do not recall her name now but that kiss I will always remember.

My Men

"If I were to list all the men I have had as lovers what you would think of me? 'She's a Slapper?' Really you should think no more and no less than you do now but sex is still such a screwed up thing in this delicate little society. Things change so rapidly one day to have had many partners might bring admiration the next scorn. I was born in1948, in 1970 I was 22 years old. I was legally an adult and could in theory do as I pleased, in practice I still lived in my parents house so when I found my first boyfriend, despite the swinging sixties, sex was not something that mum and dad were comfortable talking about. I went to the doctor and asked for the contraceptive pill. That was some discussion, he was a middle aged man and was all for calling my father up to dissuade me. I still tingle when thinking about my first time he was so handsome, thick black hair and eyes that melted into my brain I could not believe my luck that he had chosen me to be one of his conquests. Oh look at your face. You see what I mean you get all your emotions mixed up. Love and sex sure they can go together but they do not have to. I just loved it when a strong handsome young man took me in his arms and I could feel that he wanted to be inside me. There were I think just two who were not as nice as I would have liked, they were rough and I really felt as if they were with me purely to satisfy their own needs with little regard to mine. There were two who had never had sex and they got a bit to excited a bit to quickly, they had no need to be embarrassed I understood but sadly they sloped off and I did not see them again."

The Good Old Days

Lumy! We have already run out of January Fridays. I hope you realise that February can be short on Fridays, it having fewer days than most months. That is also accounting for that fact that Brexit has not only reduced the flow of exports but imports too. You can expect the cost of Fridays to rise at above the rate of inflation for the foreseeable future……Ah but come on you are not going to fool me with that old line 'Foreseeable'. That be one of the most nonsensical words available…….be honest, if the future was in anyway 'Foreseeable' life would be boring and probably not worth the living. Certainty, certainty, I maybe worrying you, but like the phrase 'as much as possible' or 'all that we possibly can'… really? ….. Have a great Friday and if we are all lucky to survive the following six days I will meet you here same time, same place for the first Friday in February..… but will it really be the same time, or the same place? Could it really be the same place..… for surely you and I, if we make it, will be another six days older, with another week of life tucked under our belts. Some dust is probably going to fall on the place before then and that will make the place a little bit different. It will not be the same time either for now is the only moment that this moment will exist and then it is gone…… Enjoy all the minutes of the next hundred and sixty eight hours, oh and make sure you don't miss any of the seconds, it is amazing what you can do in two seconds or even one. The good old days are here and they are now.

The Age Gap

He has always been six years older than me, my big brother. So when I was being born he had already been in school for over a year. I wonder if we really know anyone 'really'. I should know my big brother we shared parents, we shared the family home. We saw each other daily for the first part of my life. We went to the same primary school, but I wonder now if the six years between him starting and me starting school were such a huge gap that it could never be bridged. I have another brother who is three years older, in away that makes 'big' brother even further away. I also have a younger brother, I am his big sister by three years. I keep meaning to ask him just how far the gulf is between him and our 'big' brother. No I should not use the word gulf. There is no gap or rift when we all get together we are as close as we ever have been. Sadly though we will never be together again for my big brother passed away, it was a couple of months ago. I know the three of us who are left feel a bit rudderless now he has gone. We have been going through all the things he left behind and I really am astonished by what we have found. He catalogued so much stuff. All neatly packed in arch-lever files and with keep sakes in plastic boxes. What a life he had, he never told any of us all the details of the places he went, or of the people he met and knew. We sat around his big oak table with our mouths open. He went to dinner with presidents and went to parties with royalty. We all knew what he did for a living, but none of us had the slightest notion of what that really meant.

I Loved Acting

I had been in all the school productions since I started at the school. I think it was difficult for the teachers to find material for us but at the end of the spring term each year we put on a play or light operetta for our parents and the local dignitaries. It was difficult because it seemed to me that most of the plays and shows were made for male dominated casts. Our school was a girls school the only men in the place were two teachers who were heading for retirement and the caretaker who was in his mid fifties so there was not much place for them on our stage. For two years we did have a very talented drama teacher who wrote two musical plays which required no male actors at all. The other years most of the cast had to dress up and pretend to be boy's. I never thought it was very convincing. I did go to see a production at my brother's school and he looked just like a girl, he was the milkmaid. When I first started at the school there was no contact between girls and boys, if any of us were seen outside school talking to a boy we were in for trouble. Now I had been summoned to the drama teachers room and I was wondering if I had done something that I was to be in trouble for. No she had a huge smile on her face and she asked me if I would like to help the boys school, on the other side of the park, with their production, I said 'so long as it doesn't mean I miss out on our production.' 'No they do theirs in mid December. They are doing William Wycherley's *The Country Wife* I think they want you to be Alithea.' I said 'yes, that play is quite rude I believe!'

Romeo

We three boys could not believe our adolescent luck. We were the three in our year who hated rugby and cricket. If we could get out of it we would. Wednesday afternoon games day was the worst of the week especially when it rained and worst still if it snowed. The sporty boys gave us a lot of grief they called us names and told us we were girls and that we were gay and the rest. Of course they all tried to tell us of their sexual conquests, how they had gone all the way with this girl or that girl from the girls school on the other side of the green. We were not convinced we had all hung around the school gates hoping to even speak to one of the girls but they walked by us and would not say a word. We three we were the ones who liked to read and we were the ones who were always in the school productions. In an all boys school we were obliged to take the roles of the females, at least until our voices broke. We knew that the rugby team lads were 'all mouth and no trousers'. Then our drama teacher called us in we thought it would be about our next production but no we had an invitation to go and help with a production of Romeo and Juliet at the girls school. So for all their muscle and that wisp of hair on their chins they could never get anywhere with those girls. We three on the other hand were dropped right into the honey pot. I got three hundred Christmas Cards that year and I got to play Romeo and I got myself a girlfriend.

Ruby Red

In a solar system of a planet on the side of a galaxy there are three stars that radiate a clear blue light. That blue colour dominates that part of the universe, it enters any crack or crevice and filters through all rock and soil and liquid. Three stars in one solar system all shining in the same frequency their life giving beams. These beams are the life force of whatever they reached. They made liquids wet, deserts dry, glaciers frozen and volcano's ablaze with fire. The planets that encircle these wondrous stars are to many to easily count. Some are giants and some are pygmy. They come in all shades and variations of colour. Many have moons of multi colours. Some of the moons have moons. The largest of all these planets is ruby red and it sparkles. Once every two million years an alignment of the blue suns and the ruby red planet causes an extraordinary splendour.

Risk

"Yes they gave me a A4 size magazine with all the details and then I had the conversation with the doctor going on in my head. The magazine is a bundle of joy it first dives deep into all the things that can go wrong! If you were not feeling confident by the time you get through this page turner you are thinking is this really necessary? Wound infection, MRSA, nerve injury, deep vain thrombosis 1 in 100, pulmonary embolism 1 in 500. Then once you have been fitted you have to be careful that you do not dislocate it, it takes eight weeks for the muscle to repair and for everything to tighten up and hold the new joint together. On the bright side the doctor did say that it maybe possible to lengthen my right leg to equal the left and then I would be able to walk without limping. He said also that the new hip will last for thirty years. I laughed, I said it was great to have an optimistic surgeon and I hoped that I would out live the joint! He went over the risks of the different anaesthetic and when he had finished I said there are no risks in any of this. You have told me that unless I have this operation I will soon be unable to walk. So the risk is cancelled when do you think you can fit me in?"

Travelling Light

I was always on planes back then. British Caledonian, British Airways, Scandinavian Airways, Lux Air, Swiss, Singapore Airlines, Cathy Pacific, Egypt Air, Thai Airlines, there was one that flew to Borneo they called it the flying banana, and my favourite Emirates. I met fascinating people. In a lift at Gatwick Airport there was a man who had a button business, it is amazing what I could tell you about buttons from that one short journey. There a was woman on a flight to the Philippines who travelled the world in search of butterflies. I sat next to Muslims, Sikhs , Jews and Christians all had their tales to tell. I travelled light then and never took a bag into the cabin. I always checked it in. I had a wallet that hung around my neck and the leather strap was so long I could push the wallet down the front of my trousers. I bought that in Kenya, there were many there who tried to pick pocket and this was a good solution. In this wallet I carried my passport, money, note book and pen. I lost count of the number of cabin crew who complimented me saying "Now that's the way to travel."

Blood.

"There is a risk in this operation and it might be that if there were to be a problem you might require a blood transfusion." Said the nurse as she handed me a leaflet. Blood transfusion, I never thought that I might need one. How many litres of blood have I given over all these years. I know I have a heart badge somewhere and a certificate praising my donations. So this was one area in life I had definitely a balance in my favour. That was the way I liked it. If I climb the hill to the 'Pearly Gates' anytime soon I can say to Saint Peter well I made a pigs-ear of most of it but I did give a good bit of my blood for the injured. Now if they have to give me blood how much will they have to give? How will the books balance up now? One of the good things I managed to do in my life all upside down. Ah well at least I can look at if from the perspective that I did give and as long as I get no more than I gave at least I am even!

Accident

It was an early evening in the late summer and she was driving her *Volvo*, her daughter strapped into a child seat in the rear safe as houses. These were the military roads outside the Hohne Kaserne in the north of Germany. If there were army exercises these roads would be closed but this evening they were a short cut back home for dinner with her husband. The road was deserted but for the *Volvo* so how the accident occurred I will never know. In Germany the law required anyone who came across a road accident to stop and assist. There was a problem with the assisting bit because if you assisted and did any harm by your assistance you could be held liable! It was not unheard of that people stood gorking at an accident rather than helping the victims. Somehow the young German women had managed to drive head on into a huge beech tree and although the *Volvo* was one of the safest in the world then the woman was trapped by her platform shoe beneath the peddles a bone was sticking up out of her flesh, there was a lot of blood. I looked to the back seat the little girl was dead. We had no mobile phones in those days I got my pen knife out and cut away the shoe and as the pressure released the woman screamed in pain. The doors at the rear would not open. Then a Land Rover arrived with a couple of soldiers together we smashed the rear door windows and one of them climbed in and cut the body of the child from the seat. We took her and laid her on a blanket from my car. We carried the woman to the Land Rover and then the *Volvo* caught fire.

Lilacs

They had not long been married. All the time in the run up to the wedding things had been fun and life was sweet. The wedding was a fine affair. He should have realised that the number of friends and family from her side were many fewer than from his side. The party went well and when they left the revellers they found their car had been filled with balloons and a sign *Just Married* had been scribbled over the back windscreen in red lipstick. It was when they arrived back at the house he felt it. She turned cold and as he suggested he should carry her over the threshold she spat back that he should grow up and that she was going to bed and that she should not be disturbed. Things were not easy from that moment on. Then he went off to work one day returning mid afternoon and he found myself in total shock. The super little house which he had bought and which he had cared for a good few years before she turned up, it looked so beautiful from the front as it was framed by two wonderful lilac trees. In the spring the right one gave white flowers and the left purple. He looked and felt as if he had been in an accident and that he had lost limbs for the two lilac trees had been cut down and removed. Leaving the white house walls naked and unframed. He should have ended the marriage right there and then. He never really recovered from that.

Declamation

"Alright you have learned by heart all the words of this poem. Your diction is excellent so now we must move from that to an arresting performance, with just these words and your voice you will stand on the stage and command the audience to look to your direction so that they may hear this exciting story. So those first two words must come from your mouth like two bullets from a gun. The crack of them must capture the attention of every single person sitting in the room, go on give it a try see how you do." "The wind." "Yes not too bad funny little word 'the' easy to throw it away as a needless decoration but it brings so much to the work and is a powerful tool for you to use. You should want the audience to ask 'what?' THE WHAT, so a very slight pause 'the' half a beat and then 'WIND' put the emphasis on 'WIND'. Ok Try again." "The...WIND." "Excellent. Now they are wondering what the wind is up to what is it doing, where is it going, has it cooled something down or blown something away? They will surely be wanting to know. Curiosity it is so fine a tool. Please continue if you will." "The...WIND was a TORRENT of DARKNESS...among the GUSTY TREES." "Yes, yes you have the idea, exactly. You see how precious every word is and well done for making the end T on torrent so clear."

PB

I Had to Say

How young was I then? Not even twenty. I had the idea of being a famous singer fifteen years before that. They put me in the School Nativity Play and I thought that was wonderful. All those folk staring at me as I sang that Christmas carol and they all went ahr....They put me in all the school concerts and plays after that and I heard some folk songs which I liked so I wanted to play the guitar so that I could sing the songs too. Bit by bit you will find your way too. I had luck and fell into a 'vat' of red wine- 'The Folk Clubs'. Each weekend I would work and each night of the week I would travel here and there to see if I could get a floor spot. Eventually I got to be the resident singer in a big club it was 1972/73. One of the guys who ran the club had a small agency. I told him I wanted to earn my living with my voice and guitar and he said: "I will give you a gig for hogmanay get yourself a pal to do the gig with you, a 30 watt amp and learn some Buddy Holly numbers." To my surprise it worked quite well so the following year I was passed on up to a bigger agency. This was a real professional gig and frankly I was no where near close to making a success of that evening.

I stuck it out, I kept on going show after show. I did a bit of roadying for a guy who had a hit record and one of the musicians said to me get yourself a summer season on a holiday camp. Go and find out just what you can do with people. So I did and there I stood on a stage with a band behind me and I looked out over a ballroom that could house a thousand guests and after a while if I spoke on the microphone they stopped and they listened to me because I had learned how to make them want to hear what I had to say.

The Singer

His career had left him a few years ago. He had not wanted it too but the world got sick and everyone was locked down. It could not have come at a worse time. His age and all, he had still been working nearly everyday but it was tough. He never lost his enthusiasm nor his enjoyment of the sport of getting each new audience on to his side. School children to the ancient residents of nursing homes he knew exactly what and how to get them laughing and enjoying his show. He did not care much for the songs. He could not care less if this was the way to Amerilio or not. Nor if the green grass was really at home, nor if the beautiful Spanish eyes would wait for him. What he liked was the sport. It was a game, he was the cat pretending to be the mouse and that couple at the back of the audience, who could not settle into the show and they kept on talking. He held back, although they were disturbing the crowd, he wanted the crowd on his side and against the talkers so he waited and just at the right moment BUSH like in a magic spell he would change from mouse to cat and he would throw a comment right to them, or a crescendo, or he would rephrase a line of a song so it came to the ear with a different syncopation. He might even stop and ask a question, or let one word escape his mouth at a loud volume, or he might soften his voice altogether. It was as if he were the giant who had reached down and snatched up Jack from the beanstalk and suddenly everyone in the auditorium knew that he on the stage was the professional because show after show had taught him what they could not know unless they had done what he had done.

The AA Box

Well the other day I told you a bit about my Dad's old car. It had a starting handle. It could be that you have never heard of such a thing. Long before electric cars and hybrids, it was necessary to start cars with a staring handle, not with a key or by pressing a button, but by standing at the front, of the car and inserting a large metal rod into a hole beneath the radiator grill. The handle had three parts. The long rod that went into the engine then a shorter rod joined at right angles to the other end. Then another rod joined at right angles to the second rod. The handle was then turned to start the engine. In those days there was a troop of trusted mechanics they wore a brown uniform, with high leather boots, and a peaked cap. They scoured the highways for motorists in distress. Any motorist could join the club and pay an annual membership fee. With membership members could call upon the army of mechanics.

Each member was issued with a badge to fix to the radiator grill of their car and a key to unlock special phone boxes, which could be found around the country. If a member was in trouble on the road and they were near one of the boxes they could use their key to open the door to the box then they could use the telephone within to call for help. If an AA mechanic saw a membership badge on a car they would stand at the side of the road a salute the driver. The AA boxes were painted in black and yellow. Mobile phones mean these boxes are now obsolete. There are a few which are maintained for the nostalgia and to puzzle tourists. There is one the A708 road in Scotland. Head northeast out of the town of Moffat. Carry on for about twenty miles or so you will find it on the left. There used to be one on the A96 north of Inverurie and another between Fochabers and Elgin.

Barbie

I was in a different country actually a different world. A man for whom I had to do a job kindly allowed me to stay in his beautiful house in the tropics of Indonesia. The marble floor took one past the rattan furniture and out through the patio doors to the garden which was full of bougainvillea and a swimming pool. There was a kind lady who did the cooking and another who cleaned. There was a man who looked after the pool and another who was the chauffeur. They had been instructed to care for my every whim whilst I was a guest. Bathed in the warm sunshine in the day and cooled by the rain of the evening I was living for a few days way beyond my means. I am perfectly sure that Rosa the cook knew that I was from a very different world than her boss. I asked her about her life and where she lived, I asked about her family. After a couple of days she reluctantly agreed that I might visit her home. So the next day the chauffeur drove me to the other side of town. He then kindly waited for the duration of my visit. Rosa lived in what is best described as shantytown. People had managed to secure a space and then they built a shelter from anything they could find.

I had been in slums before. I remember the slums I saw, as a child, in London. I had been in Kibera, in Kenya, and the shacks of Manila, in the Philippines. Rosa's slum had cemented paths through it so, on the whole, it was a good place. Rosa's family home was for her husband, eight year old daughter and baby son of about one year old. They had rooms with curtain walls, the curtains seemed to be made of the covers my granny used to spread on top of the bed during the day time. They had their television and radio so there was electricity. There was a tap over a sink. They stuck photographs onto *Gordon's Gin* bottles, by way of frame. Rosa asked me to pick up the baby, although he was chubby and had a very large head he seemed to weigh almost nothing. I had picked him up using the force needed to pick up a Scottish wean, poor little thing could have shot through the ceiling! I had a present for Rosa's daughter, to me it looked like a Barbie doll, to Mary it was a huge disappointment. She told me that it was not the right make, as it was not a real Barbie she would not keep it! I hope it was just her disappointment speaking and that once I was gone she played with and gave it some love.

A Breathe of Air

It feels such a long time since I was a little girl. I was one of the truly lucky ones. I had a father and mother who were totally wonderful and I was housed, fed, washed and clothed everyday of my childhood. I did have some challenges and the doctor, a kindly man, who seemed as ancient as a god and looked like one too, I thought, tried his very best to help me. I woke this morning with the problem that I have endured for all the years I can remember. I loose sleep and feel tired because of it. It is not so bad now from one point of view, the asthma which used to suffocate me when I was a child is much, much, easier as an adult. As a child I used to breathe through my mouth most of the time as my nose was ever blocked and no amount of blowing into handkerchiefs could clear the passages. I did discover one relief for me was cold air.

The frozen food section of any supermarket back then had rows of open freezers and just standing in the ally and breathing in the cooler air was wonderful. So if my mum and dad were going shopping I would be sure to go as well. There were so many nights in my childhood I lay awake trying to get enough air into my lungs. The doctor gave me a medicine it was light green, transparent and tasted like the air from an inner tube of a bicycle tyre. These days if I cannot sleep it is because my nose is blocked and no amount of blowing into a tissue can clear it. It is hay-fever season once more but I sneeze at things all year round it seems. I have often wondered if it is the fault of my body that I am allergic to things or is it the fault of the air I breathe? Whatever I am an old woman now and I have managed to breathe, one way or the other, all my life. I suppose that is good and I am happy that I have!

Loon and the Moon

Where I come from a boy is called a LOON. That is but one letter away from MOON. In those days, of the 1960's, when the Russians launched a man into space and the Americans did so too, they chased to reach for the stars and I was captivated by the idea. My granny gave me plastic model kits of the rockets and spaceships. I wrote to NASA and they sent back to me beautiful pictures of the 'Prime Crew' of each Apollo mission. By that time I had already watched Ed White do the first 'Space Walk', Gemini 4, on the television news, I sat with Granny and Granddad and watched. Oh a long time before that, when they launched 'Telstar', we saw the first television pictures that it relayed all the way from America. In 1969 I stayed up all the night and I watched Neil Armstrong. I heard him say, "I'm at the foot of the ladder", he said that the luna surface appeared powdery and then, through the crackle of radio, as he stepped onto the surface of the moon he said "That's one small step for (a) man, one giant leap for mankind." Did he say the (a) or was it lost in the crackle, I do not think anyone watching cared.

Some of us watching had the picture, sent to us by NASA, of the Prime Crew of Apollo 11. We watched Buzz Aldrin and Neil Armstrong, we saw the American Flag and heard President Richard Nixon squirming his praise, over the telephone, from the 'Oval Office'. (Thanks to Alexander Graham Bell, an Edinburgh man, of course.) I and many others, looked at the photograph and saw Michael Collins, the other member of this team and we thought of him alone in the 'Columbia' awaiting the 'Eagle' to return from 'Tranquillity Base'. We watched the splash down. We watched as these three men travel the world to tell the tale of their great adventure. When they came to London I was a wee loon living in this foreign land. I held my Dad's hand. We stood, with a huge crowd in Downing Street, outside 'Number 10'. A car arrived, camera flashes lit the area, as if in a thunderstorm. We saw three men alight the vehicle, Neil Armstrong, Buzz Aldrin and Michael Collins and we were just a few meters from these men who had been to the moon. I have never forgotten that since I were a wee loon.

Use Your Vote

It is election time in my country. Democracy has its chance today to progress. Only a few will hear the call of the ballot box. Many will think what is the point I cannot make any difference? To them I would say how would you like me to write my next novel missing the page where, finally, all is revealed? Your vote is as important as that page in the book. I just had a discussion about <u>one</u> word in my next book. The editor was all for changing <u>one</u> word 'their to his'! However, that one word change. Would have rendered the title of the book null and void and half of the possible culprits would have been eliminated before the reader had read the first paragraph! We live in a world where there are many people who want to be top of the pile and those sorts of folk are just looking for a pile of other folk to climb on top of as they ascend, they never understand that without those they are climbing over there would be no top.

Democracy is challenged all the while; it maybe that other systems, yet to be invented, will be better that it. At the moment the alternatives are displayed as dictatorship. The lack of a substantial opposition is such a problem. A legitimate government needs a strong opposition to make it truly credible. If none exists the race through the election to power did not even have to be run, so how could the victor legitimately claim the victory? I am not a fan of football but I guess there are teams from around the world who are so well known I could use them in this analogy. Suppose 'Manchester United' or 'Real Madrid' took their best squad of players to the park next Sunday, and they played a match against some school kids, what would be the glory of a win for the big shot professionals? So until we have a better, support Democracy at every turn because the alternatives are truly less pleasant. Your vote is a page in the book and the story will hardly be recognisable without your page.

Changi

It was always great to travel through Singapore Changi Airport. I thought anyone could loose themselves in there for days and never get bored. It was dark when we landed, on this occasion I needed a hotel room for a few days. As a child I had been a great fan of speech radio, I was never one for the pop music. What I liked were plays and stories. They took the 'school-boy' me around the world, in company of heavy weight writers. My head was full of South East Asia because of them. I really did not know who Somerset Maugham was but I did hear many of his stories played out on my transistor radio. After my great grandfather past away I inherited a radio from him. The stories took me to Singapore and to The Raffles Hotel. Never did I dream that I would be able to stay in such a grand, in my mind it was grand, hotel as The Raffles. The luggage finally arrived on the carrousel so I picked up my bags and headed for customs and then passport control. Then out into the arrivals hall. There was a stand where hotels advertised, I had stayed at 'The Sea View' on my last trip to Singapore, it was a modern high-rise, I cannot recall being able to see the sea from my window. I looked down the list of available rooms. To my astonishment there was a room at 'The Raffles' and the room rate was very reasonable. I booked and headed for the taxi rank. I sat in the air-conditioned cool and imagined myself as Somerset in a Rickshaw through the tropical night. The room had two sections, an entrance with armchairs and a mini bar, then through to two single-beds. It was not that fancy really but there was the atmosphere and the idea that Somerset's ghost might appear. I had a good night's sleep, and then had breakfast by the swimming pool. In the afternoon a 'Singapore Sling' in the bar. I just had to buy a pith-helmet.

Miss You

Outside a static caravan, which looked out over the sea, he sat. He came to the campsite at Easter time, every year, and stayed until September evenings began drawing in. When I say 'every year' this was the first year he decided to do this but he was certain that he would do this from now on until he died. The caravan had always been in his life. His parents bought him here when he was a boy. In those days he would venture down to the beach and search the rock pools at low tide for hours on end. His wife died last year it was a huge loss for him. They met when they were fifteen and neither looked at another person romantically, in all the years they were together. They just got along, they were never stressed by what the rest of the world did. The first time they went on their holidays together was

Glasgow Fortnight 1972. The weather was really very good, but it would not have mattered if it had been rain or snow. To be away from the tenement for a while and soak in the sea breeze was nothing short of wonderful. That was, coming on, forty-nine years before. You can do a lot in forty-nine years, he thought to himself. The sun poured down upon him and soaked through his white hat. He always wore a hat to keep the sun at bay in the summer and to keep his head warm in the winter. Winters are not what they were he thought to himself. He stood up and went inside the van to make a cup of tea and to cut a slice of cake. He baked good cakes and bread. He looked at the photograph of his wife and him sitting together by the caravan where he now sat alone. He looked at the picture and into the eyes of his departed wife and he said out loud, "I miss you."

For Sale

"It has been on the market for five years. As you can see the property is spacious in this fine rural setting the hills in the background, horses in the field over there yet just ten minutes drive to the town where everything you could need is available, I would say that the price is a steal." "Well you would, you are the Estate Agent, what else could you say? Why has it been on the market for five years? Is what I am asking myself. Suppose I decide to sell it later will it take me five years? I have bought and sold a number of houses. You know what has always puzzled me? I have never left a house without removing all my personal effects, and having cleaned everything to spotless. Yet every house I have bought has always been full of the previous owners flotsam and jetsam, along with their filth. I have to say this place is amazing for it looks like the people woke up, got out of bed, grabbed a cup of coffee, and some cereal, and then left without making the beds, or doing the washing up. Look there is a towel hanging on the side of the bath, in the child's bedroom there are clothes left on the floor in a heap, someone obviously hoping that someone else will scoop them up and put them in the washing machine. Look at the cup on the kitchen worktop it has mould growing on it in layers, you should wrap that up and send it to a laboratory, it may contain the cure to a great many illnesses. I tell you what it looks like to me is as if the Sheriffs Officers came one morning and evicted the previous occupants. So the property comes complete with all this garbage, plus all the stuff in the shed. There is the damp in the porch and the wall behind the back kitchen. It will be a huge effort to make this habitable but the property seems sound enough. So I will offer twenty-five thousand under your asking price." "It's a deal." Smiled the estate agent. Then the strangest thing. Not one half hour later the estate agent called on the mobile: "You will never believe this. I have just had another offer on that property. Twenty thousand more than your bid." My response was this: "No I do not believe you I was born at night, but not last night. Sell it to them."

Expensive Education

I suppose I have retired, but maybe not. I have been around I have seen lots of things, I have been to lots of places but I realised again today that there is always something new to learn. Learning always costs. It was an expensive day! I read a joke the other day; I do not know who made it up. 'It went so: 'What makes a shoe mender think he can mend watches, do engraving and dry cleaning too.' The place, near me, where they mend shoes, mend watches, do engraving, dry cleaning, cut keys, they also put new batteries into car keys. So now we get to it. For several days, these past weeks, I have been working around my house and in the garden. When finished I have put my dirty clothes in my washing machine. The other day I forgot to empty my pockets and so I washed my car keys!

Strange but once dry the little buttons that will open the doors no longer functioned. That made the car difficult for the tailgate does not open with the normal key. So I found the spare key and used that until I washed the spare key too. Today there was time to get to the shops. The man who does the repairs told me to return in fifteen minutes. I did. He said that both keys worked and the little light flashed as he pressed the buttons. The first key did as he had said. The second key failed to perform. I watched him use a knife to clip off to plastic cover of the key he put his thumb on the flat battery, slipped the plastic cover back on and then asked me to pay a sum that was enough to melt a credit card. If it ever happens that I wash my keys again I will change the battery myself!

Hedgehog

"My Lords, Ladies and Gentlemen." The circus ringmaster raised his black top-hat and it circled in the air above his head. His welcoming announcement faded into the big-top then he bellowed once more. "Now all the way from London Town we have the most remarkable young woman, the one and only 'Human Cannon Ball'. Please clap your hands and cheer for Zazel." The band played the introductory music the entrance curtain swung away and the bunch of clowns acrobat-ed into the ring making a great fuss of pushing and pulling, falling over each other as they dragged the cannon into the light…. "Yes Daddy." Said a bright-eyed girl of ten years, her blonde hair in plats on both her shoulders: "The circus was brilliant. I have never had such fun." Her father asked what was her favourite part?

"My favourite part? It is so hard to say. I think the funniest part was the hedgehog. I mean no one would have expected that. Zazel she is so brave. I do not think I would dare. It was spectacular, the flash as the gunpowder fizzed and the bang, my ears nearly fell off! Then she was flying across the circus ring and into a net followed by what everyone thought as a ball. Somehow Zazel turned and caught it and I could clearly see Daddy, it was a hedgehog! I mean did Zazel make the hedgehog apart of her act on purpose? Or did it somehow crawl into the cannon before the show? Or did someone find the hedgehog and put it into the cannon? If someone did that how did they know it would not get hurt, or ruin the explosion, or make it dangerous For Zazel? What do you think Daddy?"

Come Back

He was such a sweet little boy. Nobody tells you what it is really like. We went to the anti-natal classes. Well that was a waste of time, for the delivery room is a world away from that musty church hall and the young excited couples, all soon to be first time parents. Oh boy the pain of allowing a child out of my stomach and into the light of day, sorry I miss wrote, it was three in the morning when they could finally, cut the umbilical-chord. That was just the beginning. A little forewarning of the nightmare and tribulation of the world as a parent would have been a much better use of our time rather that the stuff about home-births, water-births and: 'your job dad's is to rub your partners back!' Rub my back! I remember screaming to him keep away from even touching during that labour! 'Natural-child-birth', give me a break. (One couple from our group had a child stillborn, it does not get much worse than that.) Yes I know you cannot help but love the being you have given birth too, well maybe not everyone feels that way, I certainly fell in love with him, I wonder if that made Bill, my husband, jealous, maybe he was, maybe he wasn't, he is certainly nowhere to be found now, he left years ago. That little mite too, the one I carried for nine months, the one I loved, fed in the night, washed, clothed and sent to good school. No end of toys, fun and the books I read with him. Then the teenage temper-tantrums and all of a sudden university. Maybe I should not have paid his keep, in Scotland the tuition is paid by the state, maybe I should have made him work his way. Where is he now? My wee sweet one? I do not know. What was it I did to be left so alone? He is ever there inside my head living, breathing and being. Yet he has no longer anything to do with me. I see the photo of his beautiful baby-face and if I could time-travel I would go back to find the love of that wee-man. My wish is that the telephone would sound, it would be him and I would ask what I did to make him leave and say I did not mean too, whatever it was. Come back to your mum my son, I love you.

Fortune

I saw a picture of some little people dodging bombs in Syria. Not long after that I saw a photo of my family on a summer holiday, so many moons ago. There was my mum and dad and my youngest brother and sister, I guess my other brother was taking the photograph for he was not in the picture. What struck me was how smart we all looked. They used to say dressed in 'Sunday best'. I suppose that was because people used to dress up to go to church. My Dad was in a suit with a tie at his collar, Mum was in a very nice frock with a white hat on her head. My sister had a dress and a white cardigan. My brother in his shorts and shirt, and me in my jacket and trousers. That was us, on the promenade, by the seaside, probably 1968. Toby, my youngest brother was four years old then. All four of us have had a good try at living; we have all found some economic success.

None of us has suffered under bombs. We have all been lucky enough to eat, drink and sleep under a roof most days and nights over all these fifty years. What fortune to be born here and not there, what fortune to be born into a part of the world where there are always things to eat. I have managed to feed my children too, they are all grown and gone on their way now. I look back on what my parents did for me and my brothers and sister, I am not sure how they managed it all but then I am not sure how I made it either. I still like to be dressed smartly, to wear a tie jacket and smart trousers. I really wonder how the people survive in war torn places and for that matter, how those who live here, who have been less fortunate than I, manage without the start my folks gave to me.

Taste

The trouble with tasting something really good, for me, is that that memory flavours all subsequent tasting-s of similar items. I will present several examples. However before I do I must tell you I am not moaning just saying. I am content that I had these special moments and although I long for them once more, I at least have had the wonderful memories to ever enjoy. Of course I also know that some people are not in as fine a position as I, or have not made the opportunities which I have managed to make for me. Once between Luxembourg and Trier I stopped my car and purchased a bunch of grapes. It was harvest time, those grapes were plump and green they were the sweetest I have ever known. No grape since has come close. One day I will return to that place to try and relive that moment. Then in Barcelona not far from the Clot subway there was a normal, everyday, Catalan grocers store, the nectarine was an Emperor of these fruits. Oh and whilst we are in Barcelona the Caracoles restaurant, go if you can. At the Hong Kong Football Club, things have changed in Hong Kong I do know, but back in the day, 'Fried Ice Cream with Chocolate Sauce'. I never tasted better orange juice than in the Hong Kong Hotel and two drinks from Mombassa Lime Juice and Passion Juice. Maybe someone remembers *Cydrax* or *Peardrax*, still popular in Trinidad and Tobago, I better add a trip there to the bucket list. In London *Express Dairies* used to sell a chocolate milk drink called *'Micky'*, that was a treat. In Germany there is the *Landliebe-Kako-Milch* and in Switzerland *Heide-Drink-Schokolade*. Luxembourg has a really good chocolate milk too and in Belgium the *Delhaize* super-market. As we are bathing in chocolate milk right now, The British Forces NAFFI had a great one, which came from Denmark, but on my trips to Denmark I found it not. Ok enough or this will turn into a novel. PS Did I mention Fried coconut from Manila?

Bramley

When we used to get the big *Bramley* apples from the tree, where we had the tree house, there were lots and lots of them, my father would store some of them very carefully side by side in the dark cool room that was used as the food store cupboard. It was a room off the garage. When the house was built it would have been a stables but the horseless carriage had taken over. My brother and I were not too keen to be sent to the cupboard for supplies as occasionally a mouse might be seen and although we were both a *million* times bigger than any mouse the mouse still had the ability to frighten us! The apples would in one way or another end up on the dinner table. Applesauce, apple pie, apple crumble. There was a time after her trip to Austria that mum made a lot of apple-strudel, sometimes it was just stewed apples. We all had to help with the washing, the pealing, the removal of any maggots. We would have a jam jar or two around the kitchen full of sweetened water. Dad would make a hole in the lid and the wasps would be attracted in through the small hole but then they were stuck because they could not find the way out. In those days there were so many wasps it seems that these days they are not as common, certainly not where I stay. Another way of cooking these big *Bramley* apples was to bake them. We would wash them and then remove the apple core with a special tool. It was made of metal with a wooden handle the metal formed a circle which had a cutting edge which could bore a hole about the size of an apple core. It was really a circular knife which could be pressed down on the top of the apple to cut through the skin and out the other side. The coreless apples were then placed on a greased baking tray, cloves were pushed into the apple skins, and brown sugar was poured on, around, and about them, and into the hole where the core had been. Mum would put the baking tray which had a shallow pool of water in it, the tray was then placed into the oven. Whilst they were baking mum would make custard, thickening boiling milk with custard powder and sugar. After twenty or thirty minutes the apples where cooked and so they were then distributed for us to eat with the custard, which was poured all over them. sometimes a battle with the skin of the apple it being more robust that the apple flesh. Not everyone liked the cloves but my dad told me once that if you have a toothache biting on a clove can bring some relief. It is said that in the Maluku Islands (The Moluccas), where cloves grow, every time a baby was born a clove tree was planted. If they grow Bramley apple trees as well they would have an extra winning combination.

Nineteen Years

I suppose I knew him better than I thought, well maybe he thought that our relationship was deeper than I realised at the time. Looking back I owed him an enormous amount for it was he who had bought people to my new business, and he and them were the people who actually got it properly started. I did really like him, I considered him to be a friend. It is just that I did not realise, until that moment, just how much I meant in his life. It was early on a sunny Sunday morning, the restaurant and shop were not really open, but I was there cleaning, tidying, preparing the brunch, which is what started each week of the business. The first time he came to the restaurant there was a big crowd of young folk, it was a birthday party. He arrived in an open top car with several, good looking young women draped across the passenger seats. He was obviously well known and very will liked as the crowd surged about the car and he hi-fived many of them. From then on each mid-week he and a bunch of his closest associates would arrive at the restaurant and spend the evening eating, drinking and playing a mysterious board game which I would not dream of trying to explain because I never understood it. On this fine morning he stood in the doorway silhouetted by the morning sun looking a bit like the Archangel Gabriel. Once he stepped into the shop and he had apologised for being so early it being before opening time, I could see it looked as if he had had very little sleep. Although he looked tired he was so full of excitement he looked as if he would burst like an over filled balloon. He could hardly speak and when he did manage to annunciate he tripped over his tongue trying to tell me of the glory of what had happened to him the night before. He told me that he had been out and he had met the most amazing women he had ever encountered. They had immediately fallen deep in to conversation and after a walk by the lake they had gone to her apartment and spent the whole night making love. He said to me: "I want you to know it first. She is the girl I will marry." I asked if had told her that! He laughed, I smiled. Six months later they were married, it is their nineteeth wedding anniversary today.

Holiday for Everyone

That wizard looked me right in the eye and he said. "Ok young man you win. You solved the puzzle and as promised I will grant you one wish. Be careful now before you speak because I wish to know not only what you will wish for but I also require to know why you wish for this special thing that you want so much. Think before you speak." I looked at the wizard's long white beard and his tall pointed hat. He pulled his cassock about him and sat down on a large throne like chair, all covered in satin and painted in gold. He stared back at me. I said: "There are loads of religions these days and they all have their special holidays. There are those that are familiar to most people and then those which are only known to the group who worships 'whatever' god they follow. What I would like to see is one day…. Now hang on wizard I want to explain properly you must not go granting my wish before I have finished, because we must get this absolutely right, so not until

I say OK?" The wizard nodded. I continued: "That we have one day in the three hundred and sixty-five and a quarter days of each year when everyone in the world no mater what religion they follow, no matter what colour, or sex they are, no matter if they are tall, short, fat, or thin. No matter if they have six children or no grandchildren. No matter if they are rich or poor, can speak three languages or they can tell you where they were when John F Kennedy as assassinated. Weather or not they ate ice cream last Tuesday. I would like one day in the year that was universally respected as a holiday celebration. I think it could draw all people together rather than be pushed a part, one day a year to remember we are all humans despite our differences. Now the day I will pick will have to alternate each year to be fair to each of the world's hemispheres. So one year it will be mid June the next mid December. So, here it comes OK….. I wish that the entire world should celebrate and have a holiday to rejoice that we are all humans, every year from now on, together on the Summer Solstice one year and the Winter Solstice the next.

Sparrow

The flock of sparrows used to live at Evo's house, the small house on the corner. They lived in the privet hedge which acts as the fence between Evo's house and the road. It is very quiet there are only a few of us living in this place now. Most of the folk up and left when the mines were closed and their houses were pulled down. The people who stay here now are the remnants of that close-knit society which is now all but gone. Actually Evo died a couple of years back but in the minds of the rest of us it will always be Evo's house even though Simon lives there now. We cannot complain about Simon, although an incomer, for he has done his best to become one of us. Very handy man to have around, he hired a tractor late last summer and cut all the grass and weeds that had sprung up, on the vacant land where the old houses had been. It made such a difference to the place, it made it look cared for again. There is no one else here with the skill or resources to do what Simon did. He just gets on with things. There was an eyesore of a shed, it had been a wreck all the days I have been here, a couple of weeks after Simon moved it there was a big bonfire and the shed was no more. He has made a splendid job of the front garden of Evo's house, really tidy now, smart mowed lawn and roses in the borders. He has put a fountain in the middle, that's a braw bonny thing to watch. He also cut the privet hedge. The shape is now a perfect oblong and the sparrows were appalled. If you walked by them, when Evo was there, suddenly this mass of green would erupt as a great flight of sparrows ascended in a great gush from the greenery. Simon had gone too far, I think that is what the sparrows chirrup to each other. They have moved out of Evo's privet and they now live in my leylandii. That is fine by me, they are such cheeky little things. I put some food for them and they swoop down, almost before I have walked away and gobble, gobble, gobble until the crows arrive and the sparrows scatter. Then magpies are there, the crows and the magpies squabble. When the herring gull arrives they all leave him to it but as soon as he is gone whoosh the sparrows are back.

Reality

It was really when I was about five years old. A tiny girl in a big school, well it seemed big to me then. I am sure if I went back there today I would see just how small it all was. That is something which is very strange but like so many things the world is not straight, things are not, necessarily, linier. I do not know if you remember reading Plato's 'Symposium'. Now I have read it, but it has been a while, I will not claim to know it word for word. I still have my copy. (Years ago when I had some excess funds I belonged to 'The Folio Society'. This was an organisation which sold books at very high prices, so beautifully bound with a hard outer box cover and lovely illustrations. Books which were made to be treasured as their content was created to be treasured.) Sadly, for me over the years most of those I bought have found homes in other peoples lives, as I gave them as gifts. I still have 'Symposium' and Kipling's 'Just So Stories'. Often I think of something I read, I know where I read it and I search my shelves only to remember I gave the book to someone, sometime ago, how long ago I do not recall. Sometimes I have given the book away and replaced it with an Ebook copy, this is seldom successful. I still have the Folio edition of 'Symposium'. It is quiet a short volume and I have thumbed through but I cannot see the bit I want. It was to do with a line between to points drawn in the mind and line drawn on paper. Two kinds of knowledge 'illusion' and 'belief'. Physical objects with their shadows and imperfections and perfect lines drawn in the mind. Well something of that order (You can correct me If you want.) Time is not one minute after another and it is not perfect. I know this well although I have a good memory I do not remember everything that has happened in my life. When I think of myself as a tiny schoolgirl I am back there in full Technicolor in an instant. Time is here and now and back then all at the same time. That is not the only strange but also 'reality'.

Bye Bye

For my money *Carol Bayer Sager* has been one of the greatest writers of pop songs in my lifetime. I am not sure if she had 'a greatest hit', she had so many hits and which was better than another well that, I suppose, is an individual taste thing. *A Groovey Kind of Love* may be her best-known song, you even hear *Phil Collins* warbling that in the supermarket as you pick up a bag of frozen peas, or as you rummage through the 'late date but still fresh section'. Carol had help in the writing of those great numbers *Melissa Manchester, Marvin Hamlisch, Neil Simon* are the names of some of them. *When I Need You* she wrote with *Albert Hammond.* Leo Sayer had a huge hit with it. Do you remember the *James Bond* Film '*The Spy Who Loved Me* 'where '*No Body Does it Better*' was the big number, Carol wrote that one too. I will tell you my favourite song of hers, I like it because it has crazy lyrics and a bouncy melody. The story line is full of irony, it is tongue in cheek but it tells us of a time, many of us have lived through. The moments when the world is falling apart around the ears, the moment when all the aspirations that you had had, only a little while before, are as a pile of sawdust on the floor. You know that you are fed up, sick to the back teeth and you are at the point of throwing an object across the room at the person you had not so long before professed to love. Now you cannot understand what reason that person ever gave you to make you feel that way. You are hot, cold, angry, sad and you want that person out of your life, you finally pick up that empty cup, that they could not be bothered to wash-up and you launch it into the air of the apartment on a trajectory, which you are hoping against hope, will hit the person you used to give your love to, full-square on the chest, as you scream at the top of your voice, only to pause and hope you have not disturbed the whole neighbourhood. They pick up the last of their boxes and head down the stair and they are gone, never to be heard from again….. The Australians bought so many copies it was a number one single there in 1977. Bette Midler did well with her version. 'Moving Out Today'. What prompted this rant? My neighbours are, sadly, moving today.

PB

Garbage

It is, I suppose, although I cannot tell you for sure, that this is much the same wherever in the world you go. I have been to many places and I really have never understood why people do it, I just know that they do. I have seen it with my own eyes. In my high-school days I remember a history teacher showing a photograph of a huge pile of shells he explained that it was actually the garbage heap of the people who had lived at that place many thousands of years before. Seemingly they ate the fish and threw the shells on to the pile. I was pleased the photograph had no smell! Of course I realise it is not easy to deal with the stuff that you do not need once a product has been carried home and the item is in use. All that paper and card and bubble wrap and you know that one day you are going, probably, to need something of the like to wrap and send something to someone for birthday or something but where to store it in the meantime? In many places the local government send people to collect the rubbish, thank heaven they do, can you imagine what the place would be like if they did not? Even though they do collect there are many who choose to take the excess garbage, that old bed, sofa and television out into the countryside and leave it on the side of the road: 'someone will find it and take it' is what those sorts of people think. I have never and can never understand that. I have seen it in Scotland, England and way back on my first trip through Italy. The poor folk in Manila, in their shacks are surrounded by piles of rotting rubbish. I was reading of Mombassa and, apparently, fly tipping is a huge problem there. I remember a visit to Borneo, Brunei and looking down into the Brunei River, from the wooden streets of the Kapong Ayre, great masses of throwaway stuff bouncing on the wave, between the stilts. A neighbour of mine dug up an old carpet from his lawn, I asked him what he would do with it. He told me he would drag it over to the unused ground and leave it there. He was surprised when I said he could not and that I would take it to the cowp (dump). It took me several hours to cut into small pieces, it filled many bags. My neighbour told me that carpet had had been buried in his lawn for thirty years.

Too Hot

The man looked at me with his squinty eyes, stubble-d chin and greying hair. This man would never win the Mr. Universe competition. He lifted his worn-out cap from his balding head. The cap was thread bare at the edges and decorated with flecks of magnolia coloured paint. These decorations were made a few weeks ago when he attempted to paint the wall that forms the barrier between the world and his little house. He was unable to make much of a job of it maybe his eyes are failing him. He left great streaks and patches of blotched irregular brush strokes which were not done by design, he has not the whit of a Banksy, Picasso or Jackson Pollock and neither has he heard of any of them. His head now exposed a monk like fringe to the rear, he pulled his forearm across his forehead to remove the sweat leaking from his pores. He is always dishevelled and today he was over-heated. If he had been a car steam would be escaping from under the bonnet and a red warning light would be flashing on the dashboard.

These days there are fewer and fewer, people who speak his language. I am sure that many would have totally misunderstood the sentences he spoke through his dried mouth. Nonetheless what he said was true. He had lived all his days in this place. He was born in the house where he still lives. When a wee lad of a large family he would pinch potatoes from the field on the farm and get salmon from the burn. In the winter, he said, it was so cold and in the summer it was fine. Now, he said, you cannot rely on a cold winter, most of the time winter is mirk and damp. You really have a job to know if spring is springing. For we seem to morph straight from winter into summer. Autumn is an early extension to the gloom of winter. In the old days he said: "We'd come to the summer time, we loved the summer, my pals and I, we'd play away in the hills all the day, until right late in the evening, it is still light 'till after ten. The weather was pleasant, warm. Now it is just too hot."

The Horse that Passed Wind

We were making a film. It was a big day of filming the stars were all there were dozens of extras. They had three double-decker buses for dressing rooms there were two catering vans. As well as all the people the cameras, lighting and props there were many horses and some were pulling various carriages. The area was surround by trees and the idea was that this *set* was *Rotten Row* in London during the time of Oscar Wilde. We were there two or three days. There was a lot of work to do dressing everyone top hats and tails for the men and long dresses hats and parasols for the women. It was cold and damp, we used to wear tights under our costumes to try and keep warm but I do not think any one achieved that. There were a lot of complex walking scenes with dialog to record. Keeping such a crowd quiet to pick up the voices of the main characters required a lot of effort from the production assistants. The set was on the path way to London airport so we often had to wait whilst a plane flew over with it's roaring engines. Thirty five millimetre film required a lot of effort and everyone waited to hear: "Check the Gate" the camera man's assistant would make sure there was no dust or hair on the shutter that would then show up on the exposed film at then end of a shot. It was a dull each day too so the lighting boys had their work cut out. There were really complicated shots with dialog as horses galloped along the track. At the end of these several long days, that began around four in the morning, with the light fading we came to the final shot at this location. It involved everyone with several horses walking in one direction followed by a horse drawn carriage. Followed by another lot of horses. There was a similar set up coming in the direction. It all had to be timed so that the carriages passed by each other on the correct mark. The director wanted the last horse on the right of the frame to have it's tail so it would appear at the edge of a television screen. Similarly the horse on the left. The horse on the right was not playing the game. Re-setting the scene took about fifteen minutes and this was the fourth reset there was no more time it really had to go well, as the camera panned down the track all held their breath in the hope the lens could follow exactly, then like a crack of thunder the horse passed-wind, if someone had fired a gun none of us could have been more startled. The director cried: "Cut…check the gate…That's a wrap." Then the whole company began to laugh.

Sleeping in the Car

Sleeping in the car was never something I enjoyed but it was an occupational hazard. The drives were so long and the work so demanding. It was often difficult to arrive at destinations in time to find hotel rooms. Hotel rooms were a luxury and a breakfast in an hotel, with coffee, was always missed on those nights when the discomfort of the car seat and the chill cold of the night could not be kept on the other side of the sleeping bag. I used to carry all the kit, wet flannel, bottles of water, an empty plastic bottle for when no toilet was available. No I never liked it but sometimes, in the dark, I would find a quite place and would not really be able to see where I was. Then I would wake in the light of the following morning and find myself surrounded by magnificent countryside or a sea view. Sometimes there would be a mist clinging to the ground, or floating, eerily, between the sky and the earth. One night, in Sweden, a tire had burst and I found the wheel brace was not the correct size. It was really annoying as the car was brand new, I never thought to check it was supplied with the correct tools for changing the wheel. As luck would have it, when I woke, on the opposite side of the road, in a dip, there was a petrol station. On another occasion I had to visit a military base in Germany. Across the road and near the entrance to the base was a wood with parking and a picnic area. I had a reasonable sleep. I did my ablutions and then drove my car back onto the road. I turned left and found myself behind a small red car. Suddenly out of the drivers window came a 'wand'. German police used these at this time. The indication was ordering me to stop. I did. The policeman was very suspicious. I had new car which was not available on the German market and he had never seen before. In the back was an amplifier which he thought was a radio and he asked me if I was a Russian spy come over the communist border. He was very suspicious and told me he would call for reinforcements. Somehow, although I did not speak German as fluently as he, I was able to persuaded him to ask at the base gate, to verify my identity. The guard said:…..

Politics

This will be a political statement: - I am Scottish and I want Scotland to be an Independent Country. We have our own languages, culture and aspirations. I have lived in England, I had family and friends who stayed there. Daily the current UK Government, to my mind, slips more and more into positions which are unsupportable. 2019 The International Court of Justice ruled that the UK's occupation of the Chagos Islands, including Diego Garcia, is unlawful, the UK government have been told to hand back the islands and it has refused. The UK Government raised their nuclear warhead stockpile from 180 to 260 just when The United Nations Treaty banning nuclear weapons came into force in January 2021. Asylum seekers are treated as criminals. EU citizens, trying to visit the United Kingdom have been accused of job seeking and have been arrested, detained and returned to their home countries. The tragedy and damage of Brexit has been hidden in the Covid Pandemic. The loyalists in Northern Ireland are upset about the deal keeping NI in the EU customs union for goods. Why they are angry is unclear as the situation has made them better off financially. The UK government has decided to drop all Covid restrictions in

Engl;and, allowing people to make up their own minds if they should keep distance and wear a facemask much to the distress of 'The World Health Organisation' who felt it better to wait. Yet another dark day as they have reduced the budget for Overseas Aid from a measly 0.7% to 0.5% of gross national income. The Prime Minister claimed that that was because of the great financial debts which have been incurred during the pandemic. However, they had enough money in June 2021 to upset the Russians by sailing navy war ships close to Crimea. They have enough money to send a fleet of ships, including an aircraft carrier, to the South China Seas to rattle sabres at the Chinese. Meanwhile England is in the pockets of the shareholders, the rivers are filthy, and there is a very unpleasant racist streak rippling through the society. Many people endure life in awful accommodation and many people are homeless. If there was a war they would find money for bombs and bullets. The way that money is now produced means that a Government, with a central bank, can never run out of money because they can always print more. Even the BBC stated that these days governments simply never pay off their debts they roll it over into more bonds. I will stop, I could go on.

Roast Tatties

You need a 'dry' potato. We call them 'Tatties'. Back in the day our autumn break from school was called 'The Tattie Holidays' and we would help harvest the main crop. When I say dry I mean the flesh of the tattie should be 'dry', some tatties, when you cut them in half, have a lot of excess moisture. 'King Edward's' are good, 'Goldies' and my favourite 'Golden Wonder'. These days you could peel them and put them in the microwave to part cook them but many still prefer to boil them in a pan. It also depends a bit on how many you have to cook and how big you like them. In the microwave maybe you need four or five minutes, if you boil them longer. You are not trying to cook them through you just need to part cook them. I think the best way is to boil them. People go on about putting salt in the water, you can if you want too, I am cynical as to whether or not it adds to the flavour of the tatties. I think if you add salt the water boils at a higher temperature. It is up to you.

I repeat you are not trying to cook the tatties right through but what you want is for the surface to cook and start to go soft. When they have remove the pan from the heat and drain off the excess liquid. You can use it to make a sauce or gravy. Let the steam rise for a bit to let excess moister to escape the parboiled tatties. Then let them cool until they are cold. You should have a hot oven ready and the cooking pan should be hot and ready too. I use olive oil, some will argue for lard or goose fat. You must turn the parboiled tatties into the pan and using a spoon roll them over in the olive oil. The oven should be good and hot 220 degrees. Put the baking pan, containing the tatties and oil, into the oven. Check on them once in a while, and turn the tatties over in the pan throughout the cooking. In a little over half an hour the tatties should be cooked and crispy on the outside and soft inside. Bon Appetit.

Independent

The microwave oven was new then. New to us and it cost a lot of money to buy it. Then there was the freezer another innovation. Then your mother wanted a dishwasher. In those days some people would invite us to dinner and then tell us what we were eating was from the freezer and then tell them how long the food had been in the freezer! How they cooked in the microwave and would wash-up using the dishwasher! Showing off that all mod-cons that had been afforded. How smart we were the three of us. You, your mother and me, we had afforded these things too. I can see your little face watching the water running into the bath. Clear fresh water, the miracle that you were, you would have been a year and a half then. All gurgles and giggles and smiles. You had a sweet little face, blond hair and oh how determined you were, forever wanting more things to interest you. As soon as I put you in the car and started the engine off you would go to sleep. I admit there were many times when we drove just so you would go to sleep. You grew and were always so interested in everything. How many books did we read? All those stories. No parent owns their child. A parents job is to help their offspring to an independent maturity. Well I did that all right. You got to eighteen and off you went. Yes I know you keep in touch from time to time, its just that I put so much effort into helping you to stand on your own two feet, I suppose I really wanted to keep you here with me. A selfish thought yes I agree. I look back to my young days and communication was so much more difficult. I suppose that is what makes it harder, the phone is always on and it is always with me in these modern times. I know you are busy I know but I know that it is more than that. It is so difficult to forgive and even more difficult to forget. You know I do not know why we were left alone. She never really explained, all I can say is we were left alone and somehow we made it anyway. I know it was not always easy, but then who said it would be? Hope to see you soon. Love Dad

Midnight Swim

It is a wonderful summer here in 1976, a warm and wonderful summer. Oh it was so hot, we were young and slim, I had hair on my head and Jose did a cartwheel on the sand. We swim in the sea in the dark after midnight lit by the street lamps on the promenade and it felt like noon. Pamela splashed in the waves and then said she thought there was a jellyfish but it turned out to be a blow-up ball. Mike built a sandcastle. Jane said I wish there was an ice-cream. We had bought nothing with us. It was a spur of the moment thing. We had all finished work at eleven, I think it was Jill's idea, we just got into Mike's car and off we went. My brain has a timeline like a concertina, stretch out the bellows and squeeze them in and their am I standing on the hot beach ten past midnight, caring not tuppence that there was work come the morn. We lay upon the sand, the whole gang of us and we searched the starry sky and looked at the moon. Then Jose said 'let's swim in the nude'. There was not much hesitation before the five of us were darting about the surf in our birthday suits. It was daring to do such then, it was nothing to do with sex. We were not into alcohol or drugs. Just five beautiful young people in the bud of life. I am sure the police would have been cross if they had been about. Jose did another cartwheel and Mike said 'come on we better get back it will be after one before we get any sleep'. We did not want to leave, our clothes full of sand and shoes too. The car windows were down and the cooler night air blow into the back where the three girls sat. I sat in the front next to Mike and he drove back along the track and the main road. We tiptoed up to the shared apartment and each of us went to our rooms. To hot to get into bed I lay on top of the cool sheet and I slept. Boy was it hot next morning.

White Bread Rolls

My old mum used to make soft, white bread rolls. It was hard to stop eating them with butter. The smell of the yeast in the warmth of her kitchen, how lucky was I. She had a passion for cooking, maybe it was because of rationing during the Second World War. Our cupboards were always stocked. Many of our meals were simple fayre--beans on toast, fish fingers, mince and potato. I say simple but for some those things would have been a prince's banquet. My own weans would never go for such dishes, their mother had a more exotic taste and a deeper purse. For years I have tried to make those soft white rolls. I got really close a couple of times. I blamed the flour, the air for being to cold, the oven and my own inability to mix the dough correctly. In the times of rationing, I have a feeling, that the taste buds in Britain were severely damaged. So damaged that many people find the fullest flavour in instant coffee and tea bags. My granny gave us

Bird's Custard and Bird's Instant Coffee and to us spaghetti came from a yellow tin drowned in a tomato sauce much like the Baked Beans and we had it on toast. The first time my mum bought Italian pasta it was long and wrapped in dark blue waxed paper. It lay on the shelf for months before she made a sauce with mince and tomato. She studied the recipe and spent hours chopping onions. When we tried to eat it we were overwhelmed by the length of the strands and fooled because our mince always stuck to potato. Things have changed, and are changing. Those bread rolls, I suddenly had a thought I had tried to bake using, what supermarkets call 'dried yeast', frankly getting the dough to rise properly, well I often as not give up. Then I remembered, it takes me a long while to gather thoughts these days, 'live yeast', I found some and today, so many years since the last time I ate my mums white bread rolls, and I made them as she used to do.

Soft White Rolls

I took 42g of fresh yeast I put it in a bowl with a three desert spoonfuls of sugar and a bit of warm water. Then about 300 mils of warmed milk, not too hot or you will kill the yeast. (Remember when you make yoghurt or bread, part of the process is GROWING not cooking, you want the yeast to grow.) I put in a teaspoon of salt and about 200 grams of soft butter. I broke 2 large eggs into a cup and mixed them with a fork. I added that to the above mixture. Then I put in 750 grams of 'strong flour', bread making flour, it has more gluten in it than normal flour and 250 grams of plain flour. I mixed the above together and made a dough, the dough needs to be moist but not too runny. I left it to rise for an hour or two. I kneaded the dough, then divided the dough into balls about eight centimetres in diameter. I wiped a couple of baking trays with a little butter to make sure the bread rolls would not stick to the pan when baking.

Then I covered all with a clean tea towel and left the dough to rise once more. About an hour or so later I warmed the oven and put the dough in to cook about 180 degrees Celsius. About half an hour later it was all done. I am not one for exact amounts of this and that in the kitchen, I think some of the television cooking shows frighten people into thinking 'that they never could' do it like the stars on the screen. Have a go, after all you can always try again if you do not get it right first time. I do not remember the last time mum made these rolls and it took me years to work it out. Of course that may mean I am not that smart! Any how I got there in the end. Sorry if you are gluten intolerant or if you are a vegan. Otherwise I hope they turn out well for you if you make them, send a photo if you do.

Telegrams

Fraser loved first nights. He had been in theatre since he was a baby, carried on to the stage by his mother, he had his first role at the age of three months. These days he wondered if it would be his last first night, for he had had so many, over the past seven decades and now he was eighty, how many more could there be? Yes, not only a first night but a first night on his eightieth birthday. How would his great grandson say it? Oh yes 'How cool is that?' Fraser looked around his dressing room, so many flowers, and cards and such nice reviews from the critics who came to the preview. The only thing missing were the telegrams. Nobody sends them these days. It is all text messages, and emails, no class involved in those. So much has changed over all these years. They barely had telephones back in the day. "Some things stay the same." Fraser said to himself. It was Henry IV part I tonight. Fraser had played this part several times before. Falstaff. *"No; I'll give thee thy due, thou hast paid all there."*

Said Fraser, out loud, to himself. "I surely have paid all". He paused and looked about his dressing room. This was a proper theatre. A Frank Matcham, in the granite city, Aberdeen. 'His Majesty's' *"At first, the infant, mewling and puking in the nurse's arms. Then the whining schoolboy, with his satchel and shining morning face, creeping like snail unwillingly to school, and then the lover, sighing like furnace, with a woeful ballad made to his mistress' eyebrow. Then a soldier, full of strange oaths and bearded like the pard, jealous in honour, sudden and quick in quarrel, seeking the bubble reputation."* Fraser smiled at his face in the mirror and applied Lecher number five, and a bit of number eight, and mixed them over the wrinkles of his cheek. "Well 'as you like it' Fraser you are looking good for eighty, so how cool is that?" "Thirty minutes mister MacDonald." Shouted the assistant stage manager through Fraser's door. "I wish we still had telegrams, they were always the cherry on the cake of a first night. Break a leg."

A Way Into The Hills

Telling people about your dreams, how naff can that be? However, I had a dream last night. I just must tell you about. I was in a house. I remember the house it was one I stayed in on a visit to Indonesia thirty years ago. Although that initial vision morphed into some other house. Somehow the house was close to a railway line where there were people working and laying new track. There was an old fashioned steam train, painted blue and black and belching steam, hissing, impatiently, to move onto the newly laid rails. The house was somewhat instable. It seemed to roll about as a ship on a swell, I had to leap from a stair to a landing as the structure moved. All that was strange enough and not at all boring. The stranger part of the dream was that I had in my hands the mobile phone which I currently use. I was trying to take a photograph with it of a large, round, transparent window, that was in one of the walls of the building. The window at once gave a clear view out of the house and then, of a sudden, with no warning, offered a television screen. The window flickered between the two. When it was not a television I could see clearly out of the house to fields and country landscape, with hills in the distance and blue skies and sunshine. Then the window was full of a face, not the whole face, the face of an animal, mouth and nostrils horse like, or cow like, or maybe camel like. It filled the window. I wanted to capture the vision in a photograph but as I tried the window, annoyingly, flipped to the television screen. There was a moment, maybe two, when I think I got a clear shot. Then I managed to get down the stairs and out of the building. The labourers were building the tracks. The blue, black, and steaming train was ready to move on and towering above me was an enormous animal. It was as tall as the two-story building from which I had emerged. It was covered in black wool. A lama, an alpaca, a cow, or a horse, I am unsure. What I know is that it was camera shy and as I clicked, it vanished and suddenly the steam train whizzed by and I caught the back of the last carriage on my phone camera as it puffed off away into the hills.

Who Would Have Thought?

Who would have thought the Taliban? Who'd have thought Boris Johnson as Prime Minister of the UK? Who'd have thought floods ripping out the guts of European towns? Who'd have thought there would be enough people to vote the UK out of Europe? Who'd have thought Trump? Now, as we slow cook our world in the *Climate Emergency*, who would have thought? That is the point: people do by habit, rather than think what are the consequences of this? You should see clearly today, how twenty years is washed away like a German town in too much rain and millions of Afghan people have just climbed aboard a time ship to several centuries ago. If you live in the UK you have a democracy, you have a vote use it, stop voting for things that are bad for us. If you are Scottish vote for Independence. Who would have thought? Some of us do. Who would have thought the Berlin wall in spring 1961? Who would have thought Pandmic in February 2020?

Who would have thought Charlie Hebdo January 2015? Who would have thought Hitler in 1889? Who thinks we need a bit more thought? Believe the world is flat if you want too, it makes no difference to me. Deny that gravity keeps us all on the ground it makes no difference to anyone. Throw your plastic cup from your car window, whilst you sit waiting for the light to change, THAT MAKES A DIFFERENCE to us all and it matters, and you should not. A passing truck whips up the wind and blows the plastic cup it flies up and over, into the river and it washes away down to the sea. Away from the shore and who would have thought? That it could get caught up on the head of a beautiful sea creature? The turtle drowned. Hey but who would have thought? It is no good thinking the others will think, most likely they will not. Who would have thought? You do, because now I have told you. Thirty years have gone by since I planted three thousand trees, because they told me that things would warm up and it was a small something that I could do at the time but who would have thought?

I Do

She said "I do". In the way that most people do when getting married. He was perfect and she was so happy. Of course like most people she heard 'from this day forward, forsaking all others until death do you part.' Like most other people she had no idea what those words meant. Yes she knew what the words meant but the understanding of all that they entailed was a yet to be read book, on the top shelf of a large library. She knew what she wanted, She thought she knew what he wanted. She knew he wanted to marry her, but the question, as one looking in from the outside--did she really know what he meant by that? As he repeated the vows he meant every word, for he had found the beautiful girl that he was crazy for and now she was his, in perpetuity, until the clouds all float away and the rocks melt in the sun. Had he understood what she wanted from all of this? No of course not. She was after seeing what it was like. She wanted to see if her dreams would come true this way and she, she, wanted a baby. Sure she could have done that by involving someone else, but he suited her, good father material. So the days went rushing by them and the babies came and they rumbled over all the effort like a car rumbling over the lines on a road warning drivers slow down for a roundabout. She did her best to love him. She thought he would be fooled by her 'thank-you's'. He was not. The happy *ever-after-dance* at that wedding breakfast, twenty-five years before, was a dusty old memory now. The wedding ring clanged like the couplings between two train carriages, the inertia looking for some external force to tear the join apart. Their children had finished school, they had stuck it out, made it through. Now what was there 'From this day forward?' She said to herself. Until death do us part. Does that mean that one of us must die?

Regulate

There is a photograph of me, I do not remember who took it. I am youthful and concentrating on some work at my desk. There is a small black and white Television and a special computer keyboard, which was one of the first banking computer's and just behind was the first 'Answer-Phone-Machine' I bought. When I bought it the telephone company were not dead keen on such things. It was super smart for those times. It looked like an expensive cassette tape deck. Something that 'Akai' would have produced. There were two cassette tapes within the machine. One which broadcast the out-going-message. "Thank you for calling I cannot speak to you right now so please leave a message and I will call you back as soon as I can, speak after the bleep." This machine revolutionised my business. I was able to call it from any phone and hear the messages from wherever I happened to be. It increased the amount of business I was able to accept. Things have moved on since then. Everyone has a phone in their pocket. Often I find I am directed to 'voice-mail', as now they call it. I wonder if I am on a list that is automatically sent to 'voice-mail', a list which actually means 'I never want to speak with you again'! If I do leave a message, often it is weeks before a call is returned. My brother, I would put a bet on it, never will I hear from him unless three full weeks have elapsed since the message was left. I wonder if he is just so busy with other things and finally, when we do speak he seems so happy to talk and the conversation runs on and on. I nearly fainted a few weeks ago when I dialled and he actually answered, live and in real time. My daughter is no different. I spend hours worried that I have offended, on the previous conversation, just to realise that I used the answer-phone-machine to make my life busier, they use it to regulate their busy lives.

Ice Cream

"Look we are off to the South of France, while we are away you are welcome to stay here for the rest of the week, it will save you on hotel bills for the next few nights, just put the door key in the box when you leave." He said to me and then he and his family disappeared along the drag and out on to the open road searching for the 'Route de Soleil' and away on their holidays. I would have liked to go too of course but other responsibilities were mine at that time. I did have a few days free from the burdens of work and so I set out to explore the small German town, which was my home at least until Donnestag (Thursday), I wandered about a bit. There was a very nice park with a lake and lots of fowl quacking and swimming on the brown water. I took a stroll around the supermarket and looked in the wondrous shop windows, displays so carefully made. Woman's dresses, men's suits, the shoe shop, the shop that sold knives and coffee, and mugs and... whatever. Then I spied an 'Ital Eis' shop. I looked over each shoulder, who was watching me go into this palace? Nobody, and I did not really care anyway! This is one of the glories of German towns, the 'Italian Ice Cream Shop'. So many flavours, banana, strawberry, rum and raisin, coconut, chocolate chip etc. etc. I sat down at a table and salivated over the menu. I decided that as I had four days here I would take four, different, ices, one on each of the days. Each was a feast. The German word for the cup that they put ice cream in is 'BECHER'. Boris Becker, was, around that time 'world number one tennis champion', so the first ice cream listed was, yes, you guessed it the 'BORIS BECHER'. Then there was 'Micky Maus Eis', Erdbeer, Eiskaffee, Putbecher, Fruchtbecher, Malagabecher. So I made my choices. I had to have the Borisbecher. It was bought to my table in a huge glass with mounds of cream and two, very small, tennis rackets, made of 'Gummi Bear' and a small sphere of white chocolate to represent the tennis ball. I particularly liked the 'Malagabecher' I think that is rum and raisin. Then Spaghetti Eis, a mixed verity of flavours of ice cream compressed through a strainer, it came out looking like real spaghetti. The best though was Amarenbecher. Wonderful, black cherries in a rich cherry sauce, poured over vanilla ice cream and piled high with cream. In those days I could eat anything and nothing would hang on waistline! Maybe you know this! A great desert is HOT sour cherries poured over vanilla ice cream, you have to be quick, nice hot cherries, nice cold ice cream

The News

The news media brings us the evil and the godly acts, the reporters hear of them and write the stories. They often try to make out that a news item is really important or outrageous to engage and keep their audience. These days to become informed you click and 'their page' floods you with advertisements which are keeping the wolves from their doors giving them funds to run their lives. It is all about the money honey. Now they pipe the news into your phone and the algorithm carefully selects what to show you based on all the clicks you made before. Do be careful where you put your thumbs otherwise they will think you want to read things you will really find irrelevant. This morning as I scrolled, I came a headline 'Outrage, snail found in lettuce'. How terrible is that? The ones in my garden ate the entire crop that I had planted before any of the little plants grow to maturity. In some places finding a snail in a lettuce, purchase from the supermarket, might be considered a bonus, for some people enjoy eating snails! So maybe those people would be 'outraged' by the fact that they found only one snail, in such a big lettuce. The world is full of people in need. War, famine, fire, flood and today the news was

'Outrage, snail found in lettuce'. As if this was an event to match the first manned space flight to the moon's dark side. I did see something, I found amusing and also interesting, in real life. I do not think it made the newspapers. A few weeks ago, I drove my car to town to buy groceries, I was not looking for lettuce or snails. It was a cloudy day, dark clouds, damp, drizzle, and a chilly wind. At the red stop light I waited. I heard the chirpy noise which is there to alert blind people that the green man is showing the sighted people that it was safe to cross the road. Then in my wing mirror I caught a glimpse of a woman marching forth to cross the street. I would say a 'typical' woman from these parts of Scotland. I say that to alert you to the thought that this story was not taking place in some tropical region. The woman had dark, curly hair. She wore a blue velvet jacket and slacks. The thing that really made her standout, the thing that made this wee story a little bit remarkable was that on her shoulder, in all it's finery, of blue, red, yellow, black and white, struggling to keep purchase, on her shoulder, flapping it's beautiful wings was a Macaw.

The Children

If my children decide not to, or cannot have children, they will never know what it is to be a parent or how it is to be a parent who has all but out lived most of their usefulness. Of course there are odd times when they find there is not another solution to a particular challenge they are experiencing and for some brief moments the warm glow of 'I need you', elevates the wretched feeling of worthlessness but as the mayfly such moments are short lived. It is only right and proper of course the goal of parenting is surely to get them up and on their own two feet and off leading their own independent lives. If you are reading this at an age where your children have flown the nest you will know that from your own and from your peers experience, that children grow and then they go. Then there are others who grow and they stay no matter what parents do they never seem to want to move on. Then there are those who go but for some reason return. Ah I am just an old softie, I look at the photographs of times when mine were children, for me they were some of the best days of my life. Of course from their point of view they may have been the worst days of their lives! Hence the lack of engagement these days! I do not really think the last bit, I am just a greedy older person who has had my full and more share of all those wonderful times, still I want more. It cannot be, they are busy now doing all the equivalent things that I did at their ages. Looking back I wonder if my parents felt the same as I do these days. Too late to ask them now but I like to think I found enough time for them in the hectic times of growing a young family. I shall never know. Anyway if any of mine turn up in the next few days, I will not mention this little conversation and if they ask me 'if I have time' I will pause a moment and say 'well of course you know I am very busy with the new book, then there are all the short stories, but of course I have time for you'….because I always have and I always will.

Time

I really am too fat. I limp when I walk. How did I start to become old? I really was happy with how things were. They X-rayed the hips they said it is 'fair ware and tear'. I cannot deny I have been going at life, hell for leather, for close on seven decades. In a universe that is thirteen and a half billion years old that is nothing much. Then when you think about it Einstein taught us that you cannot create or destroy matter. You cannot create or destroy energy. So whatever you are, whatever I am, the things that make us what we are today have been around for thirteen and a half billion years. How does that make you feel? Time is a very strange concept anyway. Many people think it is linear, a straight line from birth to death. From A to Z, from one to infinity.

That is not what time does, we see a photograph and there you are ten years before. There you are at the wedding, the funeral, the graduation. You rumble through that pile of old papers and the birth certificate brings the birth of your oldest child, straight to the fore of your brain. Have you worked out what it's all about yet? Don't tell me you have, nobody has. The question is does it matter? Frankly it has not mattered to me at all, all these years. I have been too busy doing all the things I have done and concerned that I have not done enough with this time and privilege that I have had. What can I do with the next portion? If I get any more. I tell you what I think? I will stop worrying about the fat and the limp and how old I have become. You know that kind of rubbish wastes a whole lot of time I could be using on something else like writing you another tale.

House in the Country

It is a sunshine morning here. I am lucky, my house is in the countryside. There are few people who live here, they are good people, they care for me and I care for them. I opened my shutters this morning to the sound of a cockerel crowing I wonder how many folk get that treat on a sunny morning in this day and age? I lived in the town when I was a child one of my earliest ambitions was to have a house in the countryside. It only took me thirteen years to achieve that once I have started to work. I was able to stay in that house for ten years until a slight misadventure meant I could no longer make the mortgage payments. Another thirteen years passed before I could get another place in the country by which time I was married and had a family of children to support. The place was perfect to raise children, away from the madness of a life in the city. The children had dogs, cats, and horses. It was an existence that very few people have been able to enjoy. Then my wife went off with another man and that glorious life crumbled. The house was sold and that was one of the saddest days. It was as sad as the day they came to remove me from the first house, maybe sadder for it was a true paradise now it was lost. It was not an easy time. I was in my fifties then, I had to rent rooms in houses I shared with young people half my age and who had no knowledge of all the things I had seen and done. It was difficult for them to understand where I was coming from. So I found myself working, working, working. It took a little less time to come by this place, the place I stay now, it only took ten years. I live here alone. At this time my mind is that I will stay here now for however many days I have left. It is a good place and I am comfortable in these surroundings.

The Shock

"I am sorry, I have had enough, really enough. I cannot comprehend how you can stand there with your hands on your hips already to do this. You have never mentioned this before, you came to me, to me, just an hour ago. It is a complete and utter surprise and I am not willing to go along with your stupid scheme. It really makes me wonder just who you are. I am offended by who you must think I am. After all these years working in this place together. You seem to know nothing of me at all. I can tell you that I have realised, in an instant, that I know nothing of you either. Have you even begun to think about the consequences of such a proposal? Do you not understand how many people will be harmed if such were to take place. What kind of shockwave would it be to innocent people?

People who are working hard each day to survive and keep their families as well as they can. This enterprise, you say you have embarked upon, will lead to people being removed from their homes, uprooted. How could you? How could you think I would join you in this reckless pursuit. Have you no concept that things are not always about money? I will tell you now that I will have absolutely nothing to do with it. I have notified the other members of the group and you should know I have called the company solicitors. They told me that your actions are illegal and they advised me to call the police. So I will give you one opportunity to rescind the instructions, that you, unilaterally, have sent out. You must do it now, and once you have you will resign and security will escort you to get your personal belongings, you will leave the building, and then I never want to see or hear from you ever again.

Enlighten

If you have read through my short stories, or visited my web site you will know that I am a Scottish person. I am very please to be that, there is something, I think, deep in the psyche of the Scottish people that 'says' 'WE CARE'. I wonder if that is born of the terrible famines that, in some areas of Aberdeenshire, killed twenty five per cent of the population during the seven ill years of the 1690's. It was a long time ago but as the stories fade history's beat lives on. Not so long after that came, what we call, the 'Enlightenment'. It is a long story so I will say only that the ramifications changed the world for the better, all from our bonny wee shores. Scotland is, again, at the heart of something that <u>MUST</u> change the world. For otherwise all we now know will be gone in the flames of 'Climate Change'. You may wish to consider these three proposals and decide they are stupid, they might be, I do not know what you will think, I do know that there are currently many stupid ideas which dominate the politics in England and these have a catastrophic effect upon my country. So before you dismiss what I have to say think on it a while. 1 We are told that Scotland produces far more 'renewable' electricity that is required to power all the homes in Scotland. Now I realise that not every country can do that. If electricity was made cheaper than other forms of energy immediately people would switch their heating to electric. Countries not so blessed with 're-newables' could than start to change how they produce electricity. I do not know but it seems to me that would be a quick and easy thing to do to make a big difference to emissions. It would also get clever people thinking about how it could be achieved. Of course I understand that there is no magic and I have a lot more I would say but these short stories allow space is limited. 2 The waste management industry should be controlled and run directly by governments. Matter and energy cannot be created or destroyed. Humans have been very clever at concentrating things, take uranium spread out around the globe it does no harm but we gather it up and turn it into nuclear bombs and rods for power stations and fail to 'un-concentrate' them when we have finished using them. Every product which arrives on the market eventually needs to be recycled. Leaving such work to market forces will never be good enough. I would say that waste management' should be the beginning and heart of the economy. For the sake of our environment and to stop the waste of so many resources, I think this essential. It will not be long before all the now new electric vehicles will need to be recycled, and where is the capacity to deal with all those batteries? 3 We have to, with all speed, move to be 'Hydrogen' driven. Argue, please do...

Leonard Cohen

In 1972 I worked with a bunch of young women in their early twenties. We all worked hard and were friendly with one another tea breaks were always full of laughter and we shared our personal lives with one another without thought or care. Of course we did not worry about social media because there was none and thank goodness for that. I will admit that I often took the lead in our pranks I had a deep sounding voice and was a good mimic. One of the girls was particularly good at finding men to wine her and dine her but quite often they got the wrong end of stick and wanted to take matters much further than was her desire. There was one very persistent guy who kept calling her up on the staff telephone. One day she told the crowd that she really did not like the guy but could not get rid of him. She said to me: "If he calls put on that deep voice you use to make us laugh and tell him over the phone that you are my husband, that you are in the navy, you are back home on shore leave and you want him to stop pestering your wife." Well not five minutes later he did call and so I did as she asked. The poor fellow sounded really scared as I embellished what I had been asked to say with a few flourishes of my own: "If you don't keep away sunshine me and a couple of my mates will be round your gaff to sort you, I know were you live." How the others held back their laughter I have no idea but as soon as I put the receiver down they were all giggling with tears rolling down their cheeks. A few days later as a thank you for my performance she gave me a gift, I still have it, an LP gramophone record. It was my introduction to the one and only Leonard Cohen. I still have a record player. I have just looked up at the clock it is 03:50 in the morning and so I have put that record on the turn table and put the stylus down on side two, track two. Cohen's nylon strung guitar catches the inside of my ear his thumb alternating on the bass strings and his index plucking on the g string and alternating with the middle and ring working together to pluck two strings at the same time. *"It's four in the morning."* Cohen's gravel full voice beings with the lyrics and the melody a b a g b a g b a g b a with the chords wrapping around the story and the tune Gm Eb Cm7 Dm7 and I can see the recipient looking down and reading the letter: "I'm writing you now just to see if you are better." I have the volume turned right down. I could put on my headphones but I just want Cohen in the room with me but it is to early in the morning to disturb my neighbours. I cannot sleep tonight and my mind wonders around trying to pick on transitions of my life and I cannot remember the moment that I stopped working there at that place or what happened to all those girls. Where did they all go what did they do for the last 18000 days since we were all so young and fresh. Steph was one of the other girls and she gave me a novel by Leonard "Beautiful Losers" I have to say that until I read that I had lead a pretty sheltered life as far as sexual literature goes. Agatha Christie, HG Wells, Robert Louis Stevenson, Emily Bronte offered little in the way of salacious paragraphs. Leonard helped me to grow up and as soon as my hand is better, after the operation which has caused the pain which has me one finger typing at 04:15 on this October night, I will be playing Leonard's songs on my guitar again he has been with me for half a century now and I am so grateful.

Independence

It is a day when we in Scotland, who wish that we were an Independent country morn a little. It is the anniversary today of the day that we failed to gain enough votes to secure Independence at the referendum. Today many in what we call the 'YES movement', that is YES we want Independence, have begun a fresh campaign to try once again to secure Independence. The last referendum secured nothing much for Scotland. However, it did secure "English Votes For English Laws". Meaning that one outcome of the referendum was that whenever the Westminster parliament discuss laws which only effect the English. Scottish, Welsh and Northern Irish Ministers of Parliament have no say in what goes on. At the time the English political leaders made a 'VOW' that our Scottish parliament should have protections enshrined in law. The Swell Convention should have turned into law. Scotland's membership of the European Union should have been protected, by making a law putting that responsibility in the hands of our Scottish Parliament, Holyrood. It has been more than half a century since Scotland had a UK Government which it voted for. There are supporters of the current Tory Government in Westminster here in

Scotland but I and many others deplore the catalogue of reprehensible policies and laws, a list could go on for many pages. Brexit has caused huge problems for Scottish Exporters. The fact that so many EU citizens have returned to their own countries having felt dislodged means we now have not enough workers to do all that must be done. Goods for sale in our shops are in short supply. In the meantime there is a policy of 'Hostile Environment' from the UK Government to discourage refugees and economic migrants. There are many reports of violence by police towards black people. The UK Government have not worked out how to implement the Northern Ireland Protocol nor how to arrange for the checking of EU imports to the UK post Brexit. The UK Government are interested in making money for rich people whilst many, normal people, live in squalor. Some housing associations fail to invest in giving people decent accommodation. Yet they charge people a fortune to live in slum conditions. Scotland needs to have it's own Central Bank. It needs to control Immigration, Taxation, Defence, Pensions. We need to be back in the EU and be an outward looking, inclusive, and welcoming society. Where the people and their well being are at the heart of what our government does.

John

John and I were friends for so many years. We had a friendship rooted in the fact we had both pursued similar careers. He was fifteen years ahead of me but we both knew the glory and the hardship of the lives we chose, paths which most people aspire too and most people find too steep. We first met over thirty years ago and I knew him as well as he knew me. I am sure we knew each other better than anyone else knew us both. We had both had our share of unfortunate marriages, we both had the blessing and curse of legacy children and former spouses to deal with at family events. We both knew the joy of the love of those children and the pain of a child who never forgave us for the divorce. It was the roots of our livelihoods that really bound us, for there are few who did what we did and therefore there were few who could really understand what it takes. Many people watch, and many people think they could. They make snide remarks about the salaries enjoyed by people in the position that John and I put ourselves in. Make no mistake no one gave us those positions we both did what it took to get there and for all 'they' might say, without doing what we did, none of them could do what we did. We both ran out of road, as gravity pulled our good looks to the ground and our hair diminished until the make-up girl could no longer hide the bags under our eyes. Besides, although neither of us wanted to stop, it was time to let the new people have a shot. We would, like many older people stepping back from their profession, critique the new generation, watching them on the television screen whilst we sipped our coffee. 'Oh dear', we would say, as someone tripped over a mistake that should never have been made. 'Oh yes', we would cry when someone met the high-bar of competence we set. We both suffered with sore legs, I remember, a couple of times on holidays we misjudged the length of roads and how we suffered the following day. The last time we met, in a café in Inverness, John came in with his walking stick and dressed in his kilt but as he came towards the table he slipped, he fell and his head crashed into the cupboard where the teaspoons, knives and forks were kept. Like a great, old, industrial chimney he crashed as a pile of bricks to the floor.

Rich and Poor

You heard that joke about *Jeff, Richard, Elon,* and *Jared*? No I did not think it that funny either. Pioneers? Well maybe. After all man/woman has got to do what a man/woman has got to do! Break down the barriers, reach for the stars. Human kind can do it, but must they do it? In Burundi there are around twelve million people. Most dwell in the countryside they scratch a living by farming. They export coffee, tea, and are subsidised by international donors. Half the children are malnourished. This story is even worse, putting poverty aside, the 'World Happiness Report' shows many people in Burundi feel dissatisfied with their lives. The country was rated the least happy in the world. They have had a good share of civil-wars, and genocides. The soldiers have smart uniforms, and guns, and their President has a big car and many Burundian's do survive each year. The question is how do we, the rest of the human race, support billionaire space flight and poverty that allows children to starve to death? *Yuval Noah Harari*, in his magnificent book *Sapiens*, writes of the agricultural revelation, twelve thousand years ago, converted Sapiens from 'hunter-gatherers' into 'farmers'. He describes how this promised better lives for all but in reality the increased wealth in food gave rise to 'Elites', who creamed off the excess 'profits', whilst the 'ordinary' folk made more children and then had to work even harder to feed more mouths. So history continues. Populations rise and rise. Yin and yang. Rich and poor. So is it; that the only way to make a billionaire is to make a lot more poor people? Or to make a lot more people, poor? Karl Marx provided a vision of class free societies, everyone equal. In practice the ideal, fell somewhat short. The Indian Government sends rockets into space and holds and arsenal of nuclear weapons. It has almost one and a half billion people, and sixty percent of them survive on less than four dollars a day. King Ludwig the Second of Bavaria had beautiful castles built, you may have heard of Neuschwanstein, construction began in 1869. The building led him into debts of more than fourteen million marks, about ninety million Euros today but each year now one million three hundred thousand people visit it and pay fifteen Euros each to tour the splendid rooms of the palace. The real question of our time is: How do to we feed and house everyone and let billionaires fly into space, whilst we stop the world from burning up in the climate crisis? Your answers on a postcard please. I have none.

The Last Note

There was all the razzamatazz, a gala night opening. The red carpet spread up and in from the curb, up the marble stair with the brass handrails, all shining and sparkling. The press photographers snapped away at the never ending list of celebrities who alighted the stream of chauffeur driven limousines. To get an invitation to this event meant that you were a real somebody. The women in their latest fashion statements swished and strutted, the gentlemen gave rye smiles as the couples linked arms and then were swallowed by the dark door at the end of the concourse. Every once in a while the crowd, behind the photographers, cheered as a celebrity stepped up to shake the hands and scribble an autograph or catch a selfie. The woman, who's name the crowd could not remember, the one who did the arty programmes on late night television, was there trying to get a word or two, from anyone she could manage to stop, not everyone would. Eventually all the guests were safely inside, and the commissionaire closed the theatre doors. The media circus, and the crowd quietened down, some drifted off, others were determined to hang on until the stars re-emerged from the cavern of the auditorium. Excited to take up my seat I found myself next to someone I really admired but I will not tell you who. There had been a charity auction and I had put in a handsome bid but not enough to win the big prize which was to take a small role in this evenings proceedings. Malcolm just beat me to it. Just another thousand pounds and I could have been up there. There is no denying I was a bit cross about it. Malcolm and I had been rivals since we first met at boarding school. He did not always win, but he did win a lot. Now the compere stood up and introduced the finale, he also said that we, the audience, should watch out for the important role that Malcolm would play in this especially composed piece in the show. It was exciting and stimulating. Great crescendos and melodic pianissimos. I watched Malcolm closely. He sat to the left of the main orchestra, I was anxious to enjoy his part in this concerto, then, at the very last, he stood, he held a triangle aloft and he hit it with a short iron rod. The very last note of the piece.

Turning Back the Clock

"I have been looking at old photographs and some old cine film." Announced the elderly gentleman, I had never met before. He just launched into this dialog; I could feel it was directed at me. I dropped the newspaper down to the table level in the café, the one just across the road from the village green, yes the one with the duck pond and there is a small car park. The waitress brought our breakfasts to the table and asked if we wanted ketchup. The man continued. "The newspaper is full of stories about this current government, about their treatment of the less fortunate of this 'wonderful island', well *they* say it is 'wonderful', all the time on telly. I say 'wonderful' against which meter stick? Of course now I should revert to the measurements of my youth!" He gave a chuckle and the waitress handed him a bottle of HP, brown sauce. "House of Parliament Sauce, no longer made in this country!" He gaffawed. Well of course they were given no warnings, nobody told them that it was a disaster in the making, or should I put that another way, it was a message that they were not prepared to listen too. For they 'feel that'. Well you can feel all you like mostly anyone can feel, but that makes nothing necessarily true." I put a fork full of food into my mouth and chewed as he continued. He said. "You see looking back at those photos, and the cine film from sixty years ago, I saw my great grandparents. Great granddad fought in the First World War, he survived a bullet to the side of his face. My granddad and my father fought in the Second World War. They were just normal every day working folk. No vast sums of money hoarded in a private bank. Yet when I look at the way they held themselves, the quality of the clothes they wore, these pictures were made not so long after the war, they obviously lived at a much higher standard of living than some of the people who's photographs are printed in your newspaper today." I replied: "Oh it is not my newspaper, I found it on the seat." He took a sip of his tea and said: "The point I am trying to make is that I came from an ordinary family but I was never hungry as a child, now people who are working, both mums and dad's, trying to support a family find that no matter how many hours they put in the bills are always more than the money they can earn. This government are intent on turning back the clock, well by my reckoning people should be moving to the life style which was common when I was a child. Instead there are more and more queues at food banks."

Divorce

We walked from the courtroom side by side. I am unsure what I had expected. In a sense there had been no immediate change the split between us had happened two years ago. If I am really truthful it was before that. We walked down the steps and we climbed into the car. Neither of us had said a word. It was not such an ordeal in the courtroom, he told the judge that we were not enemies, that there was no acrimony between us, we just needed his approval for the details of what had been agreed between us. The judge raise several issues, he seemed to feel that the pension provision was slim, not for me, mine was fine, but for him. He had parked his career so that I could pursue mine and he had spent more than a decade as the house-man caring for the children, whilst I worked. Oh he was not just a stay at home father, no he pursued various business opportunities from home and really I was surprised at the amount the price of our house had risen, he did all the work to it. It was truly a paradise for the children with their horses and the safe open space in which they could thrive. I really did try to 'love' but I suppose we all define 'love' as we want it. I know he was not as interested in the physical stuff, he really wanted a cuddle in front of the television, not passion. I knew what I wanted at the beginning I wanted children, he fancied me and I knew he would give them to me. If the truth be known I never fancied him at all. Once the children were born, that side of things became increasingly difficult for me, I did not want sex with him. He was not demanding but I found myself unable to offer anything to him in this regard. The situation grew and grew more difficult. Although he was so patient he did interpret the situation in terms that he felt I did not love him. I did love him and will ever be grateful, I did love him and will ever more for allowing me my children and my career. Surely I had my cake and I ate it. I just did not want him to satisfy my physical needs. I am not sure how many lovers there were, it was a mistake to leave that email on the screen, I just forgot to switch the computer off. We arrived at the house. He said to me, calmly and quietly. "I will love you forever for the children we made together but I am unsure if I can forgive the rest."

Divorce from the Other Side

What was I thinking as I walked out of that courtroom? I was thinking I will never get married again, I will never let anyone get so close to me as that so they can do all of this again. I was the bottle of Coke-a-Cola, the old glass ones, with the cap you needed to prize off with a bottle opener, I had been shaken up so much, the bubbles wanted to escape but the cap just stayed fast. That was how I was, always waiting for things to turn out right. I remember that day I saw her car parked outside that house, I said to myself hold on it means nothing. It will turn out alright. We walked out and away from the judge, who was kindly worried for my pension, I was not thinking of that at all, I was thinking how? Why? Would anyone give up all that we had spent so much time building? That night, I had switched off the light, I checked the doors were locked and was about to head up to bed and I saw the glow of her computer, she had left it on again. I clicked on the computer mouse to close the windows which were on the screen and there it was, as plain as a punch to the face, his email to her, why in English? He could have written in German, it would have been more difficult for me at that time, she was fluent, and judging by his name he was too. I had known she was no longer my wife shortly after our second child had been born. What was that ten years ago? I was never one hungry for lust, but the physical expression of love was something I craved, the more it was denied the more frustration it caused. I just thought it would sort itself out. It never did. I came to the point where I was not even allowed to kiss her. It is wretched to be so rejected. She had her children, she had her career, I put mine on hold. I did have some bits of business, I mothered the children and I was a handy workman. I made the house look wonderful and I loved the horses, even the mucking out! Something in me snapped when I read the email, the lewd suggestions made. The blood rushed to my head and violence came to my thoughts but I manage to calm myself and tell myself this will pass. Cuckhold, I remembered it from that William Wycherley play 'The Country Wife', a farce from the 1600's which, could be made to work simply by using a door to mask one character from another. It shakes you when you find out that you are the Cuckhold. We drove home from the court in silence and when we arrived back home she was about to get out of the car I said calmly and quietly: "I will love you forever for the children we made together, but I am unsure if I can forgive the rest."

Imagination

"*Imagination rules the world.*" *They* say, was said by *Napoleon Bonaparte*, who was the Emperor of France for ten years plus one, in the first part of the nineteenth centaury. *Albert Einstein*, the theoretical physicist, *they* say, said, "Imagination is far greater than knowledge. Knowledge is what we now know and understand, imagination is all that will be." We imagine this and that and we all note that not everything we imagine actually comes true. Of course neither Mr. Bonaparte or Mr. Einstein were suggesting such. What they were saying however is without imagination things that have never before existed will never exist. *Jules Verne* went to the moon in his imagination over one hundred years before *Neil Armstrong, Edwin Aldrin and Michael Collins* flew Apollo 11 there. *Whilma Rudolf* imagined winning medals at the Olympic Games, even though doctors said that she would never walk, she had Polio. In Rome, in 1960, she won three gold medals, and she was the 'fastest woman in history'. *They say* that the brain cannot distinguish between reality and the things we think of deeply and imagine. So in your mind you can travel in space, you can run for gold. *Stephen Hawking* lived to the age of seventy-six. Amyotrophic Lateral Sclerosis made his body useless, however through his imagination he changed humankind's perception of the universe. He showed us 'Black-Holes' and 'Dark Matter'. Another facet of imagination, maybe the easy one for most of us is imagining all the bad, all the dark and all the evil that there could be. All the 'what ifs'. They could be positive but be honest they are not often, are they? One of my dearest friends always says: "Why not?" It is always his challenge, so that you have to tell him why something should not happen. I saw a man and women on the news. Their three year old had climbed on some pallets, left by a fence at his nursery school. He climbed on to them and over the fence and walked home. He crossed three major roads and arrived safely. Of course the parents were angry with the nursery school but that wee feller 'imagined' he could and he did. I bet he did not get to much praise. I really hope he does not 'loose' his imagination because of what happened. The fact that he was smart enough imagine and 'to-do' will never out-weigh the imagination of parents who can only imagine all the worst things that could have happened, but didn't.

Old Friends

Sue you must have known that I fancied you. You danced with me at the college ball that first year. Then Lynda told me that you 'preferred girls', I was not sure what she meant at first, she saw it on my face, we were in the refectory for lunch at the time. I finished my mouthful of French-fries and Lynda said: "You are such a dope. Sue is a lesbian!" "Oh." Was all I could stammer back. Then, after a mouthful of water, I said: "That's a shame. I think she is so very beautiful. Now you say it her dress style is quite masculine, I suppose." So we became friends, proper friends. You went off to work in some big business and I went off to write my songs. One of the reasons I thought I stood a chance in Demark Street, London's 'Tin-Pan-Alley', was because you said you really liked a song I had written, it seems a little immature reading it now but I sang it several times at your request in the refectory after a long college day, when we drank that awful coffee from the over priced vending machine. Yes I did sell my songs and that is how I have earned my living all these years. Yes that was one of mine, it was a really big hit for them. I wrote one for you and Jean, I remember just how hurt you were when she pulled out of your life. No I never sang it to you until now but seeing as it has come up in conversation I have it recorded. It was a folk duo from America who did it but their record company pulled the plug on them so it never saw the inside of a radio studio. Here I have put it on this USB stick along with the song you liked from college. That version is sung by, well actually you listen and then let me know if you recognise him. He was number four in the charts a short while ago with another of my songs. Did I ever say thank you for that magnum of Champaign you bought as a wedding present? Yes when I married the 'mad' one! Look at the consequences of that marriage, no let's not go there, disasters I do not wish to readdress! You know Sue we would have made a great team. Still we are still friends after all these years, which is a lot more than I can say about the wives who went their own ways!

It comes to us all.

(If you have been recently been bereaved you might wish to read this at some other time.)

It is true I lie about my age. I am a lot older than I will admit too. Is that a crime? I do not really care. My life has been very full. The reason for that is, I made it so. Never have I spent a minute trying to earn money just for the sake of earning money. However, I have had to run 'like the clappers' to make enough to survive, feed the dependents, keep a roof over the heads of them all and have enough to make birthdays and Christmas exciting. I have lived and worked in many different countries. I have had the fortune to have been involved with many people whose kindness has been overwhelming. I hope that I have been able to pass on some of that kindness to others. That is for others to judge, I have tried. No one knows what ill will befall them and I have had a good share of awfulness to handle, If there is something I have been good at that is standing up again each time I have had a fall. Maybe that is what they should use if ever I am given an epitaph. Speaking of epitaph's. I stay in a small community, the nearest village is small as well. So people here know one another. There are three post/mail people who deliver the mail and whoever is on the job we always pass a word or two. The concern for me is this; they have recently taken to delivering advertising material from funeral directors.

One day last week I had three different 'special offers' from three different companies who offer this service. The leaflets sometimes appear with my name and address printed upon them. Other times they do not. The question is do the posties deliver these to everyone? Or am I been singled out for my increasing years? It does not really matter of course because death is one thing in life we can rely upon. Many of us are death adverse, me included. I still have a lot of things on my agenda. Anyway today's, lavish publicity is a four-page spread, full colour, A4 size brochure. It has a perforated tear-off section which has a ready gummed edge. That part has a fill-in coupon; you can moisten the gum and fold to stick. It makes a post card ready to post back to the funeral director. Then you can take advantage of five things this firm offers. Actually there are six for you can get a one hundred pounds discount too. I found it interesting that ninety three percent of customers would recommend this service to their friends and family! So there must be a 'communication from beyond the grave' clause in the contract, which sounds attractive. The main selling pitch is that it is ONE LESS THING TO WORRY ABOUT!.....Really?

Algorithms

Algorithms are really a recipe, that is….if you add flour, yeast, water and salt, make into a dough and cook it you get bread…..if you mix flour, sugar, butter, eggs and cook it you get cake. Computers convert all of that to '0', zero. Or '1', one. The computer can sift though millions of zero's and one's and find the combination required and then, cleverly, present the answers and results in forms which humans can read and maybe understand. At the beginning though it is humans who put in the ingredients and tell the computer what results are required for particular combinations of things. It is no good telling the computer to produce fried potatoes if the computer has no potatoes or a frying pan. Computers can only do so much. So I know that it is a computer that accepted my payment for gas and electricity on the first of October and it then, kindly, sent me an email expressing it's thanks that I had made the payment. Then three days later, it happens every month, the same computer sends an email demanding the payment it thanked me for only three days before. This month a new demand was also sent by text message to my phone! The reason for this is clear to me the humans who told the computer what to do forgot the potatoes and the frying pan, that is they forgot to add the part of the recipe, which said 'send reminders after three days IF THE BILL HAS NOT BEEN PAID'. 'If it has been paid DO NOT send a reminder'. All cars, of a certain age here have to have an annual check called MOT. Mine comes up at the end of the month along with the bill for road tax. I have the money in my budget and will pay. Today came the 'kindly reminder' from the people who deal with all of that for the Government, not the Scottish, the UK Government. There are three weeks before the bill is due but a glance at the envelope tells you a lot about that Government for it has a threat right there on the envelope, TAX IT OR LOSE IT. On the letter, inside, at the bottom of the page there is a statement 'INVESTORS IN PEOPLE, we invest in people, Gold' I think that is something of an oxymoron. Of course some people will be frightened into action, the problem though is deeper, for many live scared as they have not enough despite working hard. So the algorithms are set to scare folk even more. Do you think that is good? I do not.

A Fabulous Evening

"Good evening ladies and gentlemen. It is wonderful to know that Café Moritz is full to capacity tonight. It seems like a lifetime since were last able to open our doors to you, the best patrons any cabaret club could possibly wish for." The crowd of one hundred and fifty started to clap and some cheered. The master of ceremonies smiled into the audience through the spot lights from the small stage in-front of the band. The stage was set along one wall of the café with a door either side, leading back stage. The curtains that covered the wall behind the band were red satin, there was a Steinway grand piano, white, stage right. Down stage left was a stand upon which was a fine display of white Zantedeschia, like Champaign goblets for fairies, their presence alerted new-comers that Café Moritz was no ordinary venue and that tonight would offer no ordinary variety show. The pre-cabaret dinner had begun with wild smoked salmon and chiefs special soft brown bread with golden butter. The main course was chicken in a white wine and cream sauce, with duchess potatoes, minted petit-pois and asparagus. Desert was freshly made ice cream surprise with a tangy raspberry sauce, the surprise being a meringue buried inside the ice cream. The meringues were crisp on the out side and toffee like in the centre, where diners found a further 'splosh' of the tangy raspberry sauce. The waiters had cleared excess items from tables and poured cups of coffee. The lights in the main part of the room dimmed, the band played to welcome the master of ceremonies. The band members looked so smart in their white jackets and black bow ties. The master of ceremonies wore, by contrast, a black dinner suit, with shiny lapels. He had a cummerbund about his thin waist and a white bow tie. Everything about Café Moritz was first class. The Master of Ceremonies continued "Yes so long have we been closed for the public health emergency so tonight we have an especially exciting programme for you all to enjoy. Now it is my great pleasure to introduce to you." The band played the introductory music and then the master of ceremonies announced the name of the first act. I would love to tell you who the entertainer was, however, membership of this exclusive club is by invitation only and members are under an oath to keep much of what happens entirely secret from non-members. I will say that that singer could really, really sing, no doubt you would know who it was. You really missed a fabulous evening.

The Coat Hanger

My husband and I have been running the bed and breakfast since 1976. What a summer to start the businesses. Such a lot of sunshine, perfect warm days and hot summer nights. We were full from the moment we put up the sign. Come the end of October and we were 'nicely' shattered. Washing sheets, cleaning rooms, getting breakfasts, clearing up breakfasts. Dealing with special requests. Dealing with one or two customers who had obviously come to the wrong place. When I say that, our place did not meet the expectations they had in mind. Really those kind of folk wanted a five star hotel with waiters and room service but were lacking in funds to achieve that. Most of the guests over the years have been perfectly charming. I have an address book full of names and addresses of the people who frequently return. We run a clean, comfortable, friendly, house and give our guests a good safe stay with the added bonus for them that we keep our prices down. Of course there have been moments which have been a bit difficult. There was a biology teacher and his wife, around about 1987, their son was fascinated by the natural world, butterflies, bugs, mice, screws, newts, frogs. He found endless creatures around and about the fields here. Then the public health fellow, from the local council turned up unannounced, he gave us a thorough inspection. We keep an extra freezer in the back of the garage. I was so shocked for in it he found a plastic bag, tightly tied, and with a label stating the boys name and the contents of the bag. Obviously the boy had intended to take the package with him when he left, but forgot. Wrapped neatly in was a frozen mole. Well of course we knew nothing of this, we had not needed to go to that freezer, it took some talking to calm the inspector down! Folk often leave things behind, flannel, soaps, I found a wooden leg once, the man told me on the phone that it was his spare. We try to send stuff back to folk, it often costs us. I was just finishing off cleaning yesterday and I saw on the back of the door a coat hanger. We have wooden coat hangers, they, I think, are nicer than the wire ones, I was about to return it to the wardrobe when I noticed that it was not one of ours. No indeed this was a *Rolls-Royce* of coat hangers, shaped and much broader, the wood was, I don't know but it looked expensive. I sent a message saying I would send it on. The man replied no keep it he had one of ours, it was a mistake. Anyway I have my best coat hanging on it now.

Spot Light

Many people have the opportunity of standing on a stage and looking out into an audience whose faces are washed away by the spotlights shining upon the stage. For some people it is a terrifying thing. For others it was an experience and they moved on. The first time I had that experience was when I was five years old, it was not a big stage just a few wooden boxes really, enough to raise us up so that mothers and fathers could see us as they sat on rows of toddler-chairs, knees and thighs aching. I did my bit of the Christmas nativity and I thought 'I like this'. I have never lost that feeling. For me it is the greatest of thrills. I am not one who would bungee jump or even dive from the high board in the swimming bath, I would say that I am fairly risk adverse when it comes to such dangers, I will cross the street at the traffic light even if I have to walk another twenty meters to do so. At school we did a lot of drama. We did Gilbert and Sullivan, Josef Capek, Max Frisch, John Gay, William Shakespeare, Harold Pinter. So that was all good.

It was a battle with my parents they were really against drama school. Although he did not say it, I think my father felt that many actors were very left-wing, I also overheard him say the word 'homosexual', when he was in the kitchen talking with my mother about it. Then I heard him say. 'It is not just the men.' He lowered his voice and said. 'It can be women too!' I know mum was only worried that I would be able to earn enough money during my life time, so that I would not want. I suppose all good mums have that kind of feeling. I also think it was good they opposed me, as it showed the world just how much I wanted my place. So many years ago that first appearance yet I still love it. I like the actors, the costumes, the smell of the make up. I like the way everyone has to pull together and make the performance work night after night, audience after audience. To me it is a sport. I really do not care what I am in, comedy, tragedy, musical, to me that matters not a jot. I would say a lot of the stuff I have to do is not my cup of tea but that is what the audience wants. What I want is to pull all the people in the theatre together and make them in to an audience, give them a good time. It's us verses them and I want to win every time.

Breathe it in

The prevailing wind is from the west. In the winter you really know it if the wind comes from the east, that is when the temperature really drops, even more than if it blows in from the north. Mostly the southerly wind brings warmth. Our prevailing wind is from the west and you can see it from the bend of the trees and bushes. You can see it in the bracing on fences. My grandma would say 'open the window, let the fresh air in'. She would say: 'let's go out into the fresh air'. She would say: 'breath in deep, fill your lungs with fresh air'. Then there was a teacher in school who said: "Every time you breathe in you breath a few drops of air that were breathed in and out by Julius Caesar!" At the time it struck me as a bit yucky. The wind is blowing a 'hooley', we say in Scotland, it means a wild party, or today 'the wind could, just about, knock you off your feet'. If all this wind is air that is rushing about from one place to another and this air is coming from the west I suppose it must have blown all the way from Canada. Newfoundland, Ontario, Saskatchewan, lberta. Who might have breathed this air before me? Spin the globe a bit more and it may well have been used in Russia too. Estonia, Sweden and Demark also. That brings us back to Scotland, that would be about forty thousand miles. Enough time to mix up with all the breezes from here there and everywhere. The trees and the plants will be breathing out oxygen. The rain will wash out some of the dirt. I suppose if the wind calms a while some of the dust falls to earth. Still I wonder who breathed this before me and who will breathe it after me? The truth is we are all linked to it, much the same as plugging in your iron to smooth out your clothes, we are all plugged into this atmosphere, that surrounds us. The pressure of it pushes down upon us and it changes the weather. Without it none of us would be alive. We need it yet we do so much to do it harm. The wind is from the south today, it is warm for this time of the year. Watch the second hand of a clock and hold your breath, how long can you suck it in? Whilst you are doing that can you think of some little thing you could do to improve the air about you today?

Procrastinating

Ok, I am sorry. I am not procrastinating. I have never been lost for words, or had writers block, frankly I talk too much and probably write too much as well. The reason I write so much is that I will die one day but I notice that many books live on. I have no idea if any of my stuff will live on when I am gone but it would be great if, in a few thousand years, once humans have frazzled most living things off the planet, the progeny of the few survivors who have evolved to cope in the new conditions come across the remaining ruins of my house and there buried in the ruins, near my fossilised remains, they find a copy of one of my books, wrapped in plastic totally protected from the worst storms that raged. They take it with them and their scholars decipher the contents and base a whole new religion upon it. Then a whole new civilisation erupts from that, all based upon a story I made up a couple of thousand years before. Now some of you will be thinking fantasy! That's never happened before! I digress, as I was saying, I am not procrastinating, I have just had a pile of other things to attend to. You want a list?

Oh come on! All right. Today I had some household cores, then I had to drive to the town to collect my new glasses, then I had to go shopping, I was two hours in the car going and returning from town. Then I had to unload the groceries and fill the fridge and the cupboards. After which I had to do some cooking. Then I was just going to sit down and write you a story when the telephone rang. My neighbour has some 'strange' people staying with her, she is doing another friend a favour and these two had gone off, against advice, unprepared and under equipped to walk up a hill, a bus drive away from here. There was a great panic, for one had returned without the other, they had had a row and split, deciding to take different routes from the summit back to base. Well we were all for organising a search party and calling for the police, having made a dozen phone calls to the number of the lost man and no contact. I had just laced up my hiking boots and pulled on my *Gortex* jacket when he came strolling through the door, without a by your leave, quite oblivious to the fact that because of him I had been unable to write a story for you today.

Mackerel

I was a little girl, maybe, seven or eight years old, I went on a holiday with my Granny and Granddad. Oh I do not know where it was. We stayed in a farm bed and breakfast. It was a beautiful place. Posh too there was a sink in the room and old fashioned 'Gazunder' beneath the bed. What is a 'Gazunder'? Well they used to be common place, they were for use in the night, in the days when lavatories were outside the house. Some were plain white and ordinary, others were works of art, interesting shapes and painted with pictures on the porcelain under the glaze. There were cows, horses, pigs and chickens and flies flew around the light fittings. Just down the road was a river it was in the shadow of a multi-arched railway viaduct. We stood high up on the bank and looked down at the water below. I said I would like to swim in the water and Granddad said he would not let me. He said there would strong currents and besides there would sewage dumped in the river up stream where the town was. Back then sewage dumping was not considered a problem. The next day we went to the beach.

If you have ever seen a *Susan Hughes* book, *'Lucy and Tom at the Seaside'* it was in my mind like that. There was sand and we made castles. Granny sat in a deck chair and a man came along and granddad had to buy a ticket from him for the rental. Then we queued up for a boat to go out fishing. It was a big open boat and it was packed with people. The water was totally calm, the sun shone and the 'Captain' held the tiller and we motored away from the shore. Of course it would not be allowed these days. The whole thing would be smothered in life jackets and numbers would have been limited so the ticket price would have been too high, low profit margins. The shore seemed a long away a way when the motor fell silent. Then the 'captains mate' give everyone a fishing line and hook, we dangled them over the side into the water. In a few minutes everyone had caught a mackerel fish. To Granny's horror, I insisted on taking ours back to the bed and breakfast. The farmers wife said to me. Well young woman I think it is time I taught you how to gut a fish and cook it, Granny smiled.

Lists

What will be the future? You cannot answer that question, nobody can. Yet many people are so self-assured they often make predictions. Most people live in hope that tomorrow will dawn and that they will wake to enjoy or at least cope with it. I went to the lectures on goal setting, I learned about dreams, I read *The Secret*. Think of the things you want, avoid thinking of the things you do not want. I would surely tell you that unless you do think of want you want you will not get it. Thinking about what you want makes your brain look for the opportunities which might lead to you getting what it is that you desire. Thinking is the key. Talking to yourself is also something you should consider carefully. Tell yourself that you cannot, it will surely be true, tell yourself you can, it might not happen but you certainly give yourself a better chance. The bother with the world is there are so many distractions, so many pitfalls, so many mishaps. Looking back over my seven decades it seems to me that my dreams were always strong and, all in all, much of what I dreamed came to pass. There were a lot of jokers in the pack of cards I was dealt. The jokers tripped me up, they made me go around in circles, sometimes it was a maze and it was so difficult to find the way out. I was always a part of these things, the successes and the failures. I have often thought to write a list of my failings, a list of the things I did wrong, a list of those who hurt me and let me down. That would be a bit like one of those monks, in the fourteenth century, who went in for flagellantism. No good beating yourself up, there are plenty of people ready to beat you up, if you let them. No it is, by far, a better strategy to write a list of things you would like to do, or have, because even if they do not materialise, at least, there is the fun of trying to reach the goals which could take you to your dreams. I made a heap of mistakes, I got a load of things wrong but I am still here and some of the things I did had a ring of success. I hope I have not messed up too many people on the way. I will probably never find out anyway. I better stop this and start making a list of things I would like to happen from now on. Not just for me but for everyone.

Insurance

"It's so lovely to see you Moira." June greeted one of her dearest friends in that Edinburgh 'posh' voice she had learned fifty-six years ago. June responded. "Oh it is very nice here June, I have never been in here before." The waiter gave a small cough and Moira turned to him, she realised that he was hoping to be permitted to pull the chair out little so that she could be seated. "Oh Moira, I should have invited you here before now, they do a wonderful afternoon tea. It is nice to be served by a proper waiter and to have proper napkins. They use porcelain plates and cups too." Moira sat down and made herself comfortable at the, elegantly decorated round table, a beautiful pink rose bud in the centre in a small porcelain vase, which matched the plates, cups and saucers, all designed to catch the eye. "So tell me Moira all and everything that has been going on since I saw you last." So Moira told June about her new granddaughter and the christening, about her husband Tam's mild stroke, about the care home where her father now stayed and how she wished it was possible to care for him at home but it was just not feasible she said, he required twenty-four hour a day attention and as care homes went, well it was nice. The waiter poured another cup of tea for them both and they buttered another Scotch-Pancake and covered it with strawberry jam. "Well I will not be eating dinner to night

Moira!" Smiled June. Then she continued. "Jack will be pleased, I know what he will want, stovies and if I don't eat some he will eat the whole dish full. Did you hear about Dorothy MacCulloch?" She asked Moira. From the look on Moira's face the answer was no. So June continued. "Her husband had an accident, he was in a car crash, whilst driving to Glasgow. He has a nasty cut on his forehead and a broken leg. Dorothy said he was lucky to get out of the wreck alive. Dorothy told me that on the day before the accident Findley had been trying to arrange a new life insurance policy. By all accounts the young sales person was somewhat inexperienced. Obviously when people are in their late fifties finding a life policy is a bit more difficult. He wanted to buy a 'Whole Life Policy' so that at whatever age he lives to it pays out. A lot of these life policies finish when a person reaches eighty. Findley was really shocked when sales girl said to him 'why not take a normal insurance policy? Look at it, what is the chance of you living beyond eighty?' Findley said to her. 'I don't know, but I am going to take the chance and hope! How old are you?' She said 'twenty five.' Findley said 'goodbye' and decided to look elsewhere for a policy!"

Nature and Culture

The Armageddon is upon us and mankind has got to understand the fight between nature and culture. In nature there can be nothing un-natural. Culture changes fast and humankind runs around in circles trying to keep up. COP, thousands of humans discussing the heating climate.... We must do something.... So let us say we will stop this in ten years time. Meanwhile in Bad Neuenahr-Ahrweiler the devastation is life changing. Africa is totally dry in Zimbabwe and plagued by typhoons in Mozambique. Of course it is all very well saying 'we cannot do things so quickly', 'jobs are so important', 'how do we feed everyone', 'it takes time to change', 'it costs so much money'. There in that last five words is the conflict. Nature is nature. Money is culture. Humankind did not make nature, humankind is a part of nature and has messed up nature. Now humankind uses culture to dither and delay the actions which have a small chance of delivering us from the armageddon, which humankind has made for itself. There is nothing un-natural in nature, nature is adapting, it is flooding, melting, heating and it is not controlled by humans, it is reacting to human activity.

Money was invented, in many places, in many times. Five thousand years ago the Sumerian's used barley money. Money is a human invention, it is a cultural thing and it stands no chance against the forces of nature. Armageddon, in the form of climate change is upon us and no amount of pleading, haggling, promising, loaning, granting, can deal with what is going on. *Jeff Bezos* has two hundred billion dollars in the bank and he can rocket in to orbit. In Marsabit there is not enough water to keep the animals alive to sustain the meagre lives of people who scrape a living whilst dwelling in mud huts. Humans need to reinvent money. They are doing, credit card companies and banks make tons of it, bitcoin also, however none of that helps in Eswatini. Humans have the insane ability to not think about that which is not immediate to them. In 1858 members of the houses of Parliament, in London, could no longer stand the stink of the river Thames, so they made some money to build sewers. When humans have gone money will have no value at all, but creatures that evolve, to survive new conditions, will still have nature but maybe not as we now know it.

Nothing

"You know what was so disappointing?" He asked as he learned back on the two back legs of his chair and he blew a ring of cigar smoke from his lips and watched disappear through the room. Some went up the chimney above the flames from the coal fire. "No, but I will bet several pounds that you are going to tell me Dave." "Oh come on Jimmy you speak as if I am always going on about things." "Dave let's face it you usually are! So come on then, there is no one else in the pub. Let rip." Dave swung forward onto the four legs of his chair. It had been a long cold winter, 1963. The country had ground to a halt, there were snow drifts and icicles were still hanging from the gutter above the window of the pub which was just about warm enough to sit in and sup a pint of pale ale. "Jimmy give me one of those sausages from that hot cabinet on the bar." Jimmy took a plate and a folk and took one of the sausages he had, optimistically fried, a quarter of an hour before, hoping that there would be a few people in for a lunchtime drink. As it was his only customer was Dave, who was now sitting full square at the table and had finished his cigar. He was looking far away in thoughts. Jimmy put the plate, with the sausage on it on the table in front of Dave. Dave pushed the fork into the sausage, he dipped it in the puddle of tomato ketchup and then took a bite. He chewed and swallowed. Then he said: "Jimmy these sausages you sell are really good, I like the peppery taste." "They are from the Cash and Carry Dave, their own brand, they are not sold in shops, just to the catering trade, I like them too." "I was going to tell you about my disappointment Jimmy." "So you were Dave, go on then tell me." "Well Jimmy, I have been thinking about it for a week now, I am a loyal customer of yours, I thought that we were friends. Twenty years I have been coming in here, I must be your longest serving customer. You know what she meant to me, you knew everything, you knew, you knew Jimmy. That is what is so disappointing. You said nothing."

Borneo

Since I was a child I had had an ambition to visit Borneo. Even as I sat aboard the plane I really had no idea why. It was probably because of a man called *Michael Bentine*. He had been one of the stars of the *Goon Show*, which was, originally a radio programme which was broadcasted by the BBC between 1951 and 1960. Michael left the group and went onto make several television series. I think it was watching his television programme *It's a Square World*, which ran from 1960 to 1964, Fifty-two episodes of glorious nonsense. That gave me that dream. I looked through the aircraft window and there was Borneo beneath me. The third largest island in the world covered in thick rain forest, with parts unexplored by anyone but orang-utans and the ancient head hunting tribes. Some said still haunted by the 'Brooke Family', the last 'White Rajahs'. There was a car waiting for me at the orderly airport and it took me off a long a straight road hacked out of secondary jungle. The road ripped through the forest and the remnants and leftovers of the construction were strewn either side of the highway.

We were heading towards the north of the state of Brunei. The driver told me that there were snakes, leopards and monkeys in the jungle. I kept a keen watch and I did see a buffalo. The house in which I was to stay was 'open plan'. It was surrounded by a sort of moat which was actually the monsoon gutter. It was right by the sea. Ever since I have wanted to live in a wood hut on a deserted beach with just the waves for company. The trees had been cut right back away from the property, they said it was better like that, as it meant fewer mosquitoes. The Malay people were so different from the other people I had met on this trip. The Hong Kong Chinese, the Singaporean's, the Filipino's, the expatriates. The people I was engaging with here were practicing Muslims and I was told that they would keep their distance as they were worried by the 'religious police'. Apart from that they seemed unconcerned about anything, or anyone. The call to prayer rang out from the Mosque.

The Entertainer

"I have never seen children laugh so much Janet, you were right that young man is extraordinary. When you told me about him I really was not sure what you were going on about." "A little bit more faith in your wife Peter, I did tell you I saw him do a show a Maureen Davenport's house in January. It seems that this crowd of children know him very well and every time they see him he has a new show and how he can keep their attention like he does, that is a priceless gift. Remember the disaster of last years party when you thought your amateur balloon modelling would keep them happy! Well the funniest thing about that party was your face when they jumped on you and dragged you to the floor." "Oh it was not that bad Janet." "Peter you were in trouble do not try to deny it." "Well Wendy and Phillip had that so called Magic Man, I am glad I was not paying his fee, what a waste of money even little Freddie could see how he did the tricks and that white rabbit escaped and went to the bathroom on that white rug of theirs. You are right this young fellow is worth his weight in gold." "Watch him closely he is so intent on what he is doing, he writes all the songs and the stories and how he gets them to participate and act out the plays. He told me that he does more complex shows for the older children and if he goes to do a show in a school it becomes a full blow drama lesson. He travels to many countries apparently with the drama stuff. He is just back from Hong Kong. He also does small parts on television shows. He told me that he does that because it helps him to sell the drama but he says the television work is boring sitting about all day waiting to do a few lines which amount to thirty seconds on the screen. He said he had been in France for a week making a show about the second world war. He said the trip was good, they treated him well good food and money but he really would much prefer to be singing his own songs and engaging with real live people. He sings to people in the mental hospitals as well. Extraordinary. He works a famous theatre every summer all the well know acts visit for one night-ers. He does two shows a day six days a week and says that there never is a dull moment." "He certainly has a talent you would have thought they would have given him his own show on television." "Peter I just told you he finds the television boring, He did do a series in Hong Kong he told me but that was enough apparently He was offered his own show with one of the TV companies in Scotland but he decided not to do it. He said it reminded him of the early days of his career when record producers and managers were trying to get him to sing songs he detested. He said if he had gone along with their plans he would had ended up with a hit record that would follow him like a ghost for the rest of his life." "Well he certainly knows what he is doing he has had them spell bound for a complete hour. Oh it is our turn we have to feed them now."

PB

Climate Control

I posted a story about Borneo. It was a diary entry from 1983. That trip and others were sponsored by Shell Oil. In 1983 we spoke nothing of climate change. There was no global warming. I will also confess that I had sponsorship from various oil companies. They also sponsored events which I earned fees to appear at. I will further confess to enjoying some wonderful parties paid for by oil companies. I would not agree that we should see oil, gas, and coal producers as the evil baddies in the thing we now call 'Climate Crisis'. Of course their work has bought us to this place but the generation to which I belong were happy that they did what they did as our lives were so much better, at the time, than they would have been otherwise. It was about 1986 when I first became aware of the 'Ozone Layer Depletion'. As soon as I was aware I started to do things to advertise this problem, I worked with many groups of young people around the world. At that time I owned an area of land. I decided to turn it into a small forest, it seemed to me, at the time, that the world was changing. I had watched *Thor Heyerdahl* on television. He spoke of the voyage he made on *'Kon-Tiki'* in

1947 and how the ocean was much dirtier when he was on the 'Ra' expedition in 1969 and 1970. Human kind, I have said before, has the incredible ability to not respond to danger before it is right on top of them. I would say again and I am not alone, we need to do something today. I am going to list some of the things which I am doing, I require no applause, but I would like you to do what you can. The woodland I planted is now mature, the small loch looks as if it is a naturally occurring feature. I have decided not to continue working in the way I have done. So the distances I used to drive each year I have cut by ninety per cent. I have considered changing to an electric car but the carbon foot print which is required to build each of them is spent only after about fifty thousand miles. I am unsure if there are suitable battery recycling facilities to care for the time, not so far away, when the current generation of vehicles go to the scrap yard. I hope that hydrogen cars will be available to the mass market soon. I have added shutters to my windows, and thermal blinds. I have added to the insulation of my house, and in cold weather I warm only one room with an electric heater. I have been lobbying local politicians on the subject of hydrogen and do what I can to make people aware of the possibilities of hydrogen.

I've Lost Scot

"I have lost Scot." "What was that? The line is very, noisy where are you?" "I'm in somebody's house, using their phone, my phone's battery is dead." "So you just knocked on a stranger's door and asked them if you could use the phone?" "Yes, yes, I keep on telling you people are very nice, you just have to tell them you need and bit of help and people help." "So when did you last see Scot?" "Well you know where you dropped us this morning we walked right up to the top and then he got irritable about things and said he needed to be alone. He had his map so he went one way and I went the other." "You mean you left him in the middle of nowhere? I really think you better stop talking to me and call the police. It is dark, if they have to send people up that mountain in this gale. Call them, and then call me back." The line went dead. About fifteen minutes went by. "Helen. What did the police say?" "Oh it is alright I found him I told him we should meet by the post office," he said: "I said meet by the pub. Anyway the kind man who's phone this is will drive us back to your place." "What? Helen, you use the man's phone and then ask for a lift back home?" "Oh it's not like that, he could see we are in an awkward position. The last bus has gone. He is a very kind man. I keep telling you there are kind people all over." "I agree with you Helen, but as I said to you this morning when I left you, you put yourself in some tricky situations, I am not saying that is wrong, I admire your spirit of adventure, your get up and go. However, I think what happens in the minds of many of your 'kind people' is they look at you, they assess the situation you have got yourself into and they think they have to help because they would not want to be responsible and have on their conscience your un-timely death. Really as I drove away this morning I had to keep saying to myself 'if I had not taken them they would have gone anyway'. I also thought the earlier you start the better chance of you arriving home before dark. I know the hill was only five hundred and thirty meters, but that is a fair sized hike and you really should have stayed together and cared for one another, not got into one of your stupid, bickering, fights. Does the man know it is a twenty miles drive to get here?"

To Enjoy Later

You could smell the sweetness as you stepped into the doorway. It was an old fashioned shop. The wooden door framed the clear glass window through which could be seen many of the wonderful glories which were available just a step away. On the glass of the door was written, in gold lettering, the name of the proprietor, Mr. H. Aribo. Mr. Aribo's emporium had, actually it would be far easier to list what it did not have, but it would be to confusing to point out what was not available. There were even huge stocks of things which were generally unavailable as the manufacturers had ceased production, sometimes many years before. Then I read a notice which was hanging on the wall, in a frame which matched with the door. It explained that Mr. H. Aribo had purchased licences to produce stocks to sell in his own shop, only. Wow what an idea, a magnet for the middle aged folk who could satisfy their nostalgia guzzling the retro items only available from Mr. Aribo. This place was unique and without Mr. Aribo it would not be at all.

As I stood breathing in the smell and the sight, I wondered if Mr Aribo had a daughter or son who would one day be able to continue this great business on into the future once Mr. Aribo had gone off to Elysium to sell his wares to the families of the gods and the hero's of ancient. What a magnificent feast Mr. Aribo will present when that day finally arrives. However that day is not yet and I looked at all the glories I was amongst and wondered what I should choose. There was so much choice. I jingled the coins in my pocket, my choice was limited by that. I certainly had enough for something but some of the items were way beyond my resources. Of the things I could afford today there was a whole rack right in front of my eyes. There were some of my favourite, favourites. Three I had completely forgotten but then seeing them again, the flavour washed from my brain and around my tongue as if I had just eaten the last mouthful of one of these delicacies. In the end I reached out my hand and picked up one of the bars to the left of the display. I paid my money and I took home my prize to enjoy later.

Sounds Like a Week

I was bleary eyed, just woken, on my way from my bed to the light of the day. There is something in the way the sound of the world outside my cottage enters through the bathroom window, unlike the other windows, in this sweet place. I knew exactly the sounds, the revving engine, the clatter, which would be a clatter if the bins were made of metal but as they are plastic the sound is more of a thud. My ears strained to hear the contents of the bins fall into the dustcart, the one that is clear is the bin which contains the mixed glass and tin cans. As that sound breaks into my eardrum I suddenly realise that yet again it is Friday. I question myself, how did I get to another Friday so soon? Most of my life I have hurtled down highways. North to south, east to west by car, by ship, by aeroplane, or train and I have walked. I have been on buses travelling up to China with chickens, in the Philippines I travelled by Jeepney. I have sat on the tarmac in a plane, in Deli, for hours, whilst the authorities investigated a suspicious package which seemingly had no owner and in the end we took off with the package still aboard, obviously it did not blow-up otherwise you would not be reading this.

The Covid 19 pandemic changed all of that and the realisation that the planet is being burned up by our constant movements from here to there. I went through all my keep sakes and diaries and using the maps on the computer, I tried to work out how far I had travelled during my professional career, I gave up It was far to calculate. I suppose navy folk and pilots would do more but some of my neighbours were born in this place and they have never been anywhere since. My neighbours know which day of the week it is the night before and they diligently arrange the recycling buckets along the street, to ease the work of the environment cleansing personnel. Me? I have no idea what day of the week it is until I hear those sounds breaking through my bathroom window, when it is too late to put my plastic, paper, glass, and tins out ready for collection. So I end up putting all of it into my car and driving it to the cowp—the recycling station! That, I suppose, may not help the environment! What I wanted to say is today is the day that I realised, that somewhere during the pandemic, I pulled off the highway and ended up on a 'merry-go-round', where 'oh my heavens it is already another Friday'!

High Pressure Barometer

I have no barometer. If I did have one and I had tapped it this morning with a bare knuckle, the reading would have been for high pressure and there in my mind I am right back in a physics class. The master is demonstrating how nature abhors a vacuum. He has a long test-tube full of mercury and a glass dish full of mercury. The mercury is right to the top of the tube, only the surface tension stops it spilling. He covers the open end with a slither of glass and up ends the tube. He gently puts the tube into the dish of mercury, and he slides away the slither of glass and shows it, as a magician at and children's birthday party, to my fellow students and I. We watch on awestruck that the test tube is still full of mercury and we wonder why the mercury defies gravity and stays aloft. We learn that the air about us, the gas we breathe in, that keeps us alive, has a pressure and that pressure is pushing down on to the mercury in the dish and today the pressure is high so the mercury stay's in the tube. We are bid to look out of the window we see the blue-sky, the sunshine and some frost on the roofs of the houses opposite. We get to play with plastic straws and water. Sucking water in to the straw and putting a finger on top, to cover the hole and the water stays in the tube. This morning I went out into the high pressure morning and the sunshine, wrapped in my coat and hat. I felt my shoes slide a little on the ice and I walked around then up the farm road, where I have walked many times before. Before there were sheep on this road, they would scamper away as I approached. There are none now. The farmer has closed the farm and retired. Before I would have walked right to the top of the hill, over the two cattle grids and to the top by the gate to the farmhouse. No matter what kind of pressure the air was exerting to look back down the way I had walked, was always a thrill. The sky could be full of dark clouds or the rich blue of the summer. The bottom gate was locked at the first cattle grid this morning. I could have climbed over the gate, but somehow the gate and the padlock made that idea uninviting. The sheep have gone for good. Foresters will be planting trees up there now once the old farm buildings have been demolished. In the spring when the ice is away and it is another high-pressure day I will climb over the gate and go to the top.

Felled like a Sitka Spruce

He was certainly a big man. Tall, broad and thick in the thigh. He had been taller but gravity, age and squashed cartilage had robbed him of some of that stature. He was not unduly fat but the loss of a few pounds would have done him no harm. He was not sure how much harm had been done to him in his life. He watched with horror the news bulletins of folk who seemed far worse off than he was. Although he had worked really hard all his life, he often felt he did not deserve the things he possessed. His cottage in the countryside, his fifteen year old car, even his hat and jacket. For he often saw others with fewer items than himself. Yet on the other hand there were many people who bathed in very much deeper baths of luxury. He was quite sickened by the television advertising at Christmas time, the over abundance of food and gifts on offer. Then he thought of all the jobs that were being supported by this Christmas fantasy and he knew if that fantasy were to cease many would loose their livelihoods, what misery could that be the cause of? He was surprised on this early December evening, it was already dark but he had not yet closed the curtains, to look up, from his computer, to see his neighbours gaunt face starting in at him. She tapped on the glass to draw his attention.

He got up wincing as he did so, for his right hip was really painful and his left leg was like a stick of seaside rock with arthritis written through it. When he reached the back kitchen door and opened it she told him the new neighbour had arrived and was emptying the contents of a hire van into the next-door house. The new man was all alone, she said and as she was unable to help she suggested that the big man should! He put on is hat and his outdoor shoes, he picked out a small box of chocolates, he always kept a couple in the bottom draw just in case a present was needed and a house-warming gift was obviously needed at this moment. A few moments later in the dark and the cold of the December evening he started to transport boxes from the van into the house hirpling (hobbling) up and down the steps and a conversation grew between him and the new neighbour. The new neighbour said he was twenty-eight years old and that he and his wife intended to raise a family of three children and live in this new house until the end of their lives. The big man was immediately transported back to the time he was twenty-eight with his then wife, full of aspiration and hope. His life, another two wives and various children, flashed through the computer screen of his inner eye. In his left hand was a small suitcase, under his right arm a small cardboard box. He lifted his right foot to climb the step but the toe caught under the over hang and he was felled like a Sitka Spruce. His knee hit the ground first and some how he managed to let the rest of his body weight land on his right thumb and it hurt.

New Knees

"It's just that I never expected it to come to this." "I know. I never expected it either are you waiting on a hip replacement?" "Not yet. I can tell you though if I did not have the stick to hold me up I would without a doubt fall over. I am better off than you though, I have only one stick you have two. Are you waiting on a hip replacement?" "No I had my hips done, both sides, now I am waiting for new knees. The pandemic is holding everyone up. I will tell you too that without these crutches I would be going no where. The hips have been great, that was so fine, when they gave me those, now I can hardly move again." "Don't you wish your body could be forty again? I liked forty I felt good, I'd been around a bit, I had learned some stuff. I could eat what I wanted, never did I put on weight. Last week I had to go into town, I hobbled down the high street and saw my reflection in a shop window. This huge great stomach. Where did it come from?" "Well you are not that bad, some of the folk you see are bigger than you." "I suppose so, but I am a heck of a lot bigger than I was, funny though, when I look down, it all looks fine, it was when I glanced in that shop window and saw my reflection, I was really shocked. Hat, walking stick, leaning forward with an arch in my back. I ask you! I thought I would be running full pelt until I die." "Well some are able to, others are not, it's just luck I think. The fate was in your genes when you were born!" "That's a funny idea too, they did not know about genes when I was born! So how come fate landed this lot with me?" "You are making laugh now. Yes I know what you mean. I mean if there is a god why on earth didn't he made a bladder that was big enough to see you an eight hour sleep at night?" "Yes and if evolution is so clever why could it not have evolved so broken bits get repaired?" "Good to talk with you I'll have to go my husband has loaded the car and he wants to go home for his tea." "Good luck I hope you get new knees soon.

The Shortest Day

I get excited mid December, not because of Christmas. Shall I go all Ebenezer? Humbug. No for so many of you love it. The tinsel, the crackers and the pudding. Even on a sun drenched Bondi Beech, far from maddening Christmas songs about snow and reindeer, people love it. Not every one in the world goes for the Father Christmas of the *Coke a Cola* advertisement, there are many to whom Christmas means nothing at all. For many others Christmas is the time to make lots of money. For some it is the time to give money to give a homeless person's charity so that for one day a homeless person can have a better time of it. Only another three hundred and sixty four days to wait until that comes around again. No, the excitement of mid December is nothing to do with that for me. What I love is the twenty first of December for it is the shortest of the days, in the part of the world where I stay. That also means the night is the longest and nights are not always easy these days but the prospect is that we are no longer heading down the slope to the winter, we are climbing the hill to the summer. In the summer here the nights are not so dark, sunsets are late in the evening and often there is the fortune of blue sky warm oranges and reds as the sunsets. I have written before about wishing that humanity would put aside all it's religions, and divisions, for one day a year, giving everyone on the planet a holiday on the same day each year, as a celebration that we are all alive and we made it through the previous three hundred and sixty five and a quarter days. I suggested that it should be celebrated on Mid Summers Day. I suggested that one year that should be in the southern hemisphere and the next in the northern hemisphere. I have since come up with a better plan. Let's do it twice a year. Twenty one June and twenty one December. Two days a year when we all marvel at the fact we were born and that we do have a good place to be. Would this stop war, or evil people who entrap and enslave others? Would it provide water to those suffering drought? Would it help people be less selfish? Would it help people to understand we all rely on each other and everyone should have a fair share of freedom to enjoy it? I, of course, do not know the answers to my own questions, but may be it would be an idea to give it a try.

Bonnie Wee Queanee

You will find this hard to believe, but back in the 1950's when Scottish girls in the North East of Scotland, at least, were called queanees, I really was a pretty wee thing. It is extraordinary how things have changed during my lifetime! I really think that if you were to look at the history of the time when may great grandparents were alive, maybe even my grandparents, their lives were very much the same as the lives of countless generations that came before them. When I was just a wee quean I was loved. I had many siblings and they all looked for me as well as did my mither and faither. We had no electricity and the water we pulled from the well. We stayed in a house that had been built by my grand faither. It was quite alone, in a green strath surrounded by hills. My faither kept some animals and grew what he could. There was a forest near to the rear of our but-and-ben, and there was the moss, the peat, so although winters were colder then, I suppose we had a bit more anti-freeze in our blood stream than the modern folk, we were never cold. We always had things to do. We walked to the school two miles there and two miles back in all weathers. We had no fancy clothes, but there were times when other families, from our place, gathered. Ceildh's, there was always a turnout for the highland games. My brother, Fraser, played the pipes and we all danced. Although there were some in the strath who still clung to the notion that such behaviour should be punished. My faither would have nothing to do with the kirk, especially not the Brethren. Yes we were an unusual family for my faither owned the land our house stood upon. He was a proud Scotsman who owed nothing to no one. His love for my mither and my siblings was absolute. These days I am an alt wifie. Many an awkward times befell me in these past seventy years. Two husbands who both failed to match up to my faither. I have been living in our alt but-an-ben for some years, well since my mither past. It has many of the modern features now. Plasterboard internal walls. Central heating, electricity from a generator. There is even a toilet and shower, in an extension on the side of the house. I will stay here for the rest of my life, for of all the places I have been it is the best, here I am not an alt, fat, some might say a crabbit wifie, I am a bonnie wee queanee.

A Photograph with Jimmy

So at the end of this 2021 I had a good sleep last night. I dreamt that I fell in love and that that person fell in love with me. We were in a large refectory, dining hall, it was in an American High School. There were those plastic plates with wells for different bits of food. Hamburger in one, jello in another, there was a *Twinkie* in another, a pile of raw carrot in another and to round it off a little carton of the chocolate milk that you can buy at a commissary or PX on an American Forces base. If you do not know of *Twinkies* look them up they are now escaping America and arriving in parts of Europe. In my opinion they should be avoided like one would avoid a great white shark. However, that is just my opinion, obviously millions of people like them and eat them regularly although they are held up for ridicule by those of us who would prefer to eat a shoe, as in the old *Charlie Chaplin* movie, *The Gold Rush*, where Charlie eats his. I felt like one of the Iban or Dayak people of Borneo who believe that whilst asleep their spirit leaves their physical body and wonders around and about the rain forest. My new love in the dream sat at a table with several other people. I had been charged with looking after another person, there was plenty of room for us at the table but the person I had to look after decided to sit at another table several rows to the right.

My responsibility to that person was such that I had no option but to follow. So with a parting passionate kiss and embrace from my new beau I could only go. We arrived at the table at exactly the same time as another small group. Three men in smart suits, two of them with earpieces, and curly wires drooping behind their ears. We all sat down and shuffled our food trays. Why on earth I should have had this in my mind I have absolutely no idea, I have no affiliation and no real interest. I cannot think that I have even thought about the man except when I saw him on television news or in a newspaper. Anyway to finish off this tail, or is that tale? I am sure you will know witch, or is that which? I found myself sitting at a lunch table in the, what American's call 'A Multi Purpose Room' with the former President of the United States of America Jimmy Carter. Then the idea was to get a photograph of him and the person I was hosting but would you believe it? The camera on my mobile phone was playing up, it would not work and by the time I had rebooted, Jimmy, who had been very patient, had left to go about his business. The moral is: In 2022 make sure you have all your equipment up and ready as you never know what will turn up at any moment and you never want to miss an opportunity, for although there are many opportunities, not every opportunity will suit your skill set and you do not want to miss that golden story that will set you up for life.

Something and Nothing

Did you ever wonder what there was before everything was new? I have read all about it, *Stephen Hawking, A Brief History of Time*. I read it long ago, how time flies. It was only thirteen point five billion years ago that the 'Big Bang' occurred, the event that bought you to this story. That's right, without that big bang, all that time ago, you and I would not be here to share this gentle amusement. My parents were religious people, they read to me the Bible. Although I was a babe in arms at the Christening my father gave me a bible, he signed inside the cover with love. I grew and understood why humans cling to religion but although I still have that bible it is not the centre of my world, as it would be the main anchor of the lives of many. The stories in that book in Genesis tell of an all powerful god creating everything in six days and then having a rest on the seventh. Obviously a difficult idea to square in the modern era, as people wrestle with their latest IKEA flat pack. Then if this god did manage all of everything in six days, no one will be able to tell you exactly how long a day lasted back then! Anyway enjoy believing that which you believe, as long as you allow others the freedom to believe the things they hold dear. We are fed the notion of evolution; if that idea is so smart let me ask you this…. Your body replaces all it's cells in a seven-year cycle, so every seven years you have a new body. So why has this evolution game not made it so that the new cells repair and upgrade as we go? Instead the new cells look older than the cells we already had! As well as that a slightly larger bladder and it would be possible to sleep a full eight hours without disruption. So I have thought about these things a lot over my lifetime. At night on a sun bed on a beach in Mombassa I lay looking up at the skies of the southern hemisphere. It was a perfect clear night, no breeze and the air was warm about me. The Indian ocean lapped at the white sandy beach, at the time I thought I was in heaven. I wondered as I had done all my life, if before there was 'anything' there was 'nothing' and if there was 'nothing' actually there must have been 'something' because there is 'nothing'. Anyway before that 'Big-Bang' there must have been the 'thing' that did go bang. So if that was 'nothing' it must have been that. Whatever it was it must have been pretty big. For all my non scientific musings I have come to the conclusion that there has never been a time when there was an absence of everything. There has always been something, is my conclusion. For even if you have a vacuum, there is 'a vacuum' and so 'it is', so it must be something! It really does not matter anyway for there is enough to be dealing with here and now. There is always 'something' even in the darkness, even when all is lost there is, always, 'nothing' and 'nothing' must be 'something', so there can never be 'nothing' and yet there was 'nothing' and there always will be 'nothing' for 'nothing' is definitely 'something'.

Home to Aberdeen

It was one of the Fridays in November 1983. I woke up in an old, colonial style house in Singapore. It had a veranda and balconies about the windows of the upper floor. The old white paint work was peeling here and there, there was a haze rising from the foliage in the garden bougainvillea. The bars on the windows had kept robbers and assassins at bay during the past warm night. There was the sound of a cockerel crowing over the background sounds of the city traffic. That had been the last night of a great adventure that had taken me through the tropics of South East Asia. I liked it here but obligations were calling from the other side of the world. Tony drove me to the airport at Changi, you could spend ages in there wondering about the shops there but not today, my flight had been called for the last time and I had run. Thai Airlines, the cabin crew greeted with hands in prayer, a slight bow and a beautiful Orchid for each of their passengers, it made me feel like a guest come to their home, I wanted to remove my shoes. The flight to Bangkok was a dream; I slept all the way as I had a row of seats to myself. There were some hours to wait in Bangkok but not enough time to go into town. The airport was full of colour, orchids, puppets, trinkets. We were an hour late departing and I had company now, so no sprawling across the row. Delhi was the next stop, the heat rushed into the aeroplane as the cabin crew opened the doors. There we sat for four hours. An unmarked package had been found aboard. Eventually we took off with the package still unclaimed, every passenger thinking of the Korean Air Lines 007 which had been shot down by the Soviet Union two and a half months before. Looking at the in-flight magazine and glancing up it was obvious that most people were thinking this plane maybe on a similar flight path. Anyway we made it to London Heathrow the cabin crew opened the aircraft doors and the chill of the United Kingdom splattered once more between my eyes. There was still another flight to get home to Aberdeen.

Has Love Been Good to You?

Most popular song is about it. There are thousands of books about it. It seems that films and television dramas are incomplete without it. That is I think because it is so very rare. Less rare would be the scenario where one person is besotted and the other person is not but goes along with it because it is convenient, comfortable or nothing better had arisen. Magazines gush about it and get over excited when so called celebrities fall on the rocks and part or divorce. Anyone who has had a relationship that was 'romantic' can tell you that these things are sometimes difficult. I wonder how many couples there are, or have been, that fell 'mutually' in love with one another and stuck with it through thick and through thin until they both finished their time on earth. My grandparents were a couple from the age of thirteen, my grandfather died when he was sixty-six and granny when she was eighty-two. She never looked at another man. My parents, and their brothers and sisters all had long marriages. From the outside they all seemed to be loving and caring and they all seemed to be loyal and true. My siblings and I have not had such a time. Each of us has been into battle with three different spouses. Each of us carry the wounds and scares of the battles of divorce and the harm it has done to our children. My aunt tells me it is just luck, pure luck, that you fall into bed with the person who is right for you and that you are right for them. *Zechariah* and *Shama* were orphans in Yemen. They lived in Israel since the new state began after World War Two. They were married for ninety-one years. *Zechariah* said 'This is my first and last woman and I never threw her out.' They had eleven children. If you are a person who 'found happiness' of this kind, if you are or have been in love and that person loves you equally, I am pleased for you. There is a song I like by *Rod McKuen* *'Love's Been Good To Me'.* It is sadly not a sentiment that reflects where I have come from and, at my advanced years, it is something I now no longer crave. So if you have it, cherish it, what you have is rare, and precious.

A Tribe

I read in a book that in the primeval tribe of around eighty to one hundred and eighty people everyone knew everyone else so there were no strangers in the group. In a group of fifty people there are one thousand two hundred and twenty five one on one relationships. I started my social media sixty eight days ago. In that time I have written 37 original short stories for it but there is a challenge for me. I have followed one thousand six hundred and five people in return six hundred and fifty eight people have been so kind as to follow me. Astonishingly to me I have a tribe of people now because one hundred and fifteen of my followers have taken the time to like and some have even made positive comments about these postings. I did put a lot of photographs there too, some to illustrate the stories, of course they were simple to glace at and like, but the stories people had to put a bit of their precious time into reading. So this is a thank you my precious tribe members. I have thanked some of you but it is always nice to be thanked again. I really am still trying to work out this social media stuff. You see that book told me 'everyone in the tribe knew each other' and that gossip is vital to keep a tribe together. However, my new tribe members really do not know each other, they really cannot gossip, indeed I only know each of you by your social name and the icon you use. Like all evolution we must move forward but do we really know each other? Can we know each other without ever meeting in person. American scientists say that most communication between us is as feelings. Ones 'gut feeling' was our best defence for thousands of years. So somehow I hope that you get the right message from my meagre offerings. Thanks again and who knows we might meet one day. I read in a book by *Les Gilblin*, *'How to be People Smart',* that sighted people, learn 83% of all they know through their eyes and that has certainly been a notion I have thought about a lot over the years. I have often thought that reading a book by somebody is one of the greatest ways of having a reasonable idea about who and what they are.

Jimmy

He was a big man, Jimmy, all but two meters tall in his boots. You could wonder just how he could fit into the cabin of his tractor. He did though. All through the spring and summer then late into the autumn. Then, if it snowed in the winter months there he would be out ploughing the road. Of course it does not snow now as it did when he was a boy, it was real snow back then. The farm cottage, where his dad had set up home for his family, was a farm labourers cottage, dry enough, but not warm like the big farm house. In the thick of winter it was so cold if his mother left a pale of milk in the end pantry it would freeze solid. If she left a piece of meat hanging there in the summer the flies would cover it, his dad would wipe them off just before his mum put the meat into the old wood burning stove. He was always hungry then so there was never any worry over a few flies and venison was a strong taste anyway. His dad and mum had long since past, his dad drifted off, wheezing with farmers lung and his mum died of over work. Jimmy had had fortune, when the old farmer MacKindly past. MacKindly was a widower and had no living relatives so to Jimmy's huge surprise, MacKindly left the farm, lock stock and the enormous hill behind him to Jimmy with a note saying farm it well. Jimmy did as he was told. In the old days the farm had everything barley, oats, beasts, hens. These days the hill was used to graze sheep and fatten the lambs. What with all the rules and regulations the hens had to have their own run away from everything, just to keep his hand in Jimmy also grow a couple of fields of oats, and there was the old orchard the burn cascaded down the hillside to the east of it. Despite the short summers there was usually a good crop of apples. Jimmy was all but two meters tall and he was happy.

I Wish You Still Could

When my brother and I were wee weans, and our parents were busy, one of the things they would do to amuse us was to send us on an errand to the shops. Actually each Saturday morning one of our chores was to go to the greengrocers and the butchers to gather the ingredients for the Sunday lunch. Well my dad could have easily collected these things during the Friday evening shop, but the responsibility for my brother and I would have vanished if he had. We did not know how far the shops were, it took us a while to walk and a bit longer to get back, with the burden of greens and beef to carry. Now I can trace the journey on the *Google* maps it was exactly seven hundred and fifty meters, half a mile. It says you can walk that in nine minutes but it always took us longer than that. I suppose he was about four or five years old and I was seven or eight.

One Saturday we had to go to the dairy to buy eggs too. We joked about cows laying eggs. We messed up that day, we were larking about on the way home and I swung the bag about, forgetting it contained the eggs! When I realised I decided to put the cardboard egg box into the litter bin, I do not really know way. Oh dear mum was in a rage over that. So we had to do the journey twice that day. On occasion we would both be given sixpence and we were sent off to see how many items we could buy for that grand sum. It was a sort of competition between us but in effect we usually came home with the same things. A bag of penny sweets from the sweet shop, a bamboo cane stick, from the second of the two hardware shops, a note book and pencil from the second of the newspaper shops and a bottle of chocolate milk from the milk dispensing machine outside the dairy. I have never forgotten the taste of that, you cannot buy that product now and I wish you could.

It Sounds as if Something is Broken

All in all I think many people would find this story amusing, even funny. I mean when I asked them to deliver the new toilet, rather than just collecting one from the DIY store, it seemed a reasonable idea. To get to the store is a fifty mile round trip and with all the other building I had to do it seemed that was a couple of hours better spent. It arrived when I had just popped out to blether with my neighbour. Surely the delivery person would have heard, or maybe it was him that set it down to hard, all I know is that when I tried shifting the box in through the front door it was obvious from the sound that something had been broken. I got my penknife and cut the plastic tape, what do they call that stuff? Then I cut through the Sellotape, the glue always sticks to the knife so I had to go and wash the blade. I opened the box and I wish I had not bothered, for quite a bit of the toilet had been shattered, it would not be possible to install it and there could be no repairing such a catastrophic injury of porcelain. Only last week, I bet it was the same driver, the new microwave oven had arrived with the glass door had been caved in and had shattered into what seemed like a million shards. It was difficult to send that back but the toilet came in a box at least twice the size of the microwave. I did the necessary via the computer and printed out the returns label. The instruction was to take the package to the post office pay the postage, of which they would refund a percentage and leave it there.

The first post office person said that he did not have the space to keep the parcel over night, he told me to go elsewhere. All well and good for him but for me I had to hump the wretched thing back to the car and drive further. The next post office was inside a shop. As I pushed my way through the door a woman who was toying with buying a new cigarette lighter had already opened a can of cigarette lighter fuel and it had split on her hand and the cuff of her shirt. She then tried the new lighter and managed to set herself on fire! I stood powerless under the weight of the toilet whilst the brave shop assistant sprayed the woman with a foam producing fire extinguisher. The manager then closed the shop to clean up, I and the toilet were obliged to leave. The third post office counter clerk was not prepared to take the weight from the clearly printed label which was on the box. "No, no" he said, "suppose you have put some extra stuff in that box and I do not charge you for the correct weight. No, no you put that up on my scales." Well the scales and the size of the box, which contained the shattered toilet, really were not compatible but if it made the fellow happy, it did and he smiled and said "it is lighter than is written on the label!" Well reading he had was a bit lighter due to the fact that the box was partly supported by the glass behind the weighing machine and partly by me, as I was trying to stop it tipping off the weighing machine. I had explained the contents of the box but as I laid it to rest the tinkling sound from within caused the counter clerk to say, "it sounds as if something is broken."

Numbers

Money is numbers. Numbers are easy, in comparison to everything else. Breaking the world into numbers makes it easy for the gormless to appear clever. The way society is currently set up means that things are run by numbers. What is the best song this week? It is the one that sold the most copies. Me I cannot listen to it drives me insane! The person who earns the most money is the most successful, but his daughter hates him and his wife is having an affaire. We check the fastest, the tallest, we note the smallest and we kill ninety percent of household germs; shame it is the one percent that will kill you! More is better and so the ones who understand numbers add one and one and come up with twelve. They get to be the most successful for they learn to manipulate the numbers and cheat. Think of something you purchased a couple of years ago, something that you think was good value, without checking your old receipts, how much did you pay for it?

Generally speaking we forget the price but we remember the quality and did it do what we wanted it to do. What I am trying to say is that we are fooled by numbers. Numbers do add up, they are easy and they can easily manipulated. The numbers game leads Government's to see in macro. If they can reduce the burden of social security by ten percent, wow they did well? However at the micro end of that equation their saving just dumped one hundred thousand people in to more poverty than they were in already. The books must balance cry the politicians but guess what? Next months crime statistics show a ten percent rise in robberies. Now a whole lot of other folks are suffering too as they had their house burgled. People need people, they need love, they need to be valued and feel that they have value, they are worth it. Well that is what they say on that advertisement for, I cannot remember the product, but I am worth it, my mummy told me so. You cannot put that in numerical terms.

The Three Musketeers

I was never one for joining groups, clubs or anything really. Then Hilary asked me to come along to her line dancing club. I sat and watched. There is something, I think, quite fantastic about the way a group of people can do the same thing all at the same time. Two steps to the left two steps to the right, swing the arms around, swirl about, fold the arms and do-si-do, click the fingers push forward on the right, click the fingers forward to the left. On the way home Hilary educated me as to the names of some of these moves Apple Jacks, Rolling Vine, Twinkle Step. I watched then they cajoled me to join the line and have ago. I felt so out of place, all legs and arms, I totally wanted to slip away and never return. Oh yes they were nice about it, they said all the right things about it being my first go, that I would get the hang of it the next time I came. I held my breath and I smiled but there was no way that I would be coming that way again. I thanked them for their kindness, everyone had a drink, then put on their coats and they said see you next week, the hall emptied and Hilary drove me home. She told me of all the years that she had been line dancing and how she had met Gregory, her husband, on a line dancing weekend at a holiday camp. I listened intently and wondered why I just could not find out how I could fit into such a group. There must be such comfort, a group of friends with the same interest, a group who had known each other for so long. I just could not and still cannot, there is something in me that just does not want too. Maybe it sounds as if I am stand offish or that I think myself above that kind of thing. It is not really that I just watch such groups and although I am impressed I just prefer to be me a none member of any group. Maybe I see myself as d'Artagnan to Athos, Porthos and Aramis.

Last March

It was quite a shock for me to find you there at the end of my show. A one off show in a venue I had never worked before. I had no idea you were running a theatre in a town a short distance from there. Well I had not seen you since you had that affair with my wife, you who had been the Best-Man at our wedding five years before. A funny thing about that, I do not think I ever told you this, after all it was none of my business, you were one of my closest and trusted friends, what kind of sexual preferences you had was nothing to do with me, I did however think you were gay. So when you turned up, the pair of you, that cold, grey, winter, morning and sat there on the sofa, holding hands. I had been worried all night that something bad had happened, but no there the two of you were right as nine-pence and asking me to understand. Well I could not get mad about it, frankly the marriage had not worked from the evening of the ceremony but what with one thing and another, not to mention the baby, I could see no way out. So I just bit my tongue and gritted my teeth, for better for worse, I had made a promise. I think I was very rude that afternoon after the show.

I was glad that none of my 'fans' witnessed that, it would not have left a good impression. I must have signed two dozen autographs before I saw you hovering at the back of the room. I was confused, I was disorientated and so, although I did not say a word, or make a fuss, I know I made you feel very small and I was relieved when you realised you had made a mistake by being there, the last I saw of you was your back, with that almost limp you have on the left side, passing through the theatre door and you were gone. All these years later, yes I know that I am slow, I think you were probably trying to say sorry. In my mind though I could only hear the cleaner, of the other theatre, the one from five years before, saying sorry for my troubles and how he thought it disgusting that my wife and you were to be seen together each evening in that theatre bar. There have been many times over the past thirty years I have thought about you, loosing you was worse than loosing that marriage. Today a picture of you cropped up on my computer and I made a search for your name and I was greeting (crying) to see that your funeral happened last March.

Glass-Bottomed-Boat

It was a long time ago, that is unless you have reached a good old age, let us say over one hundred. If you are only forty or thirty then I suspect it will seem as though I am speaking of pre-history. If you are even younger probably you would equate this with the time of the 'big bang' thirteen and a half billions of years ago. Time as I have often said is a tricky beast. I have photographs I took four decades ago. Oh my god he was so good looking. I rubbed that suntan-lotion on to his back and could not believe I was the girl who got to touch him. The skin on his back was so smooth and his chest was covered in hair that I loved to run my fingers through and rest my head on when we laid on the beach in the tropical sunshine. The young folk today seem to remove all their hair, except from their heads and the girls then paint on their eyebrows! I do not really understand that. The beach was white-sand and the Indian Ocean was sky-blue. We went out into the water in the glass-bottomed-boat. We peered down into the depths and saw the pretty coloured fishes and corals. We put on masks and snorkels, dropped over the side into the clear water, warm as a bath and we swam. He grabbed me and made fun as he pretended to kiss me but the goggles and the snorkels would allow it!

We could hear the other holiday makers on the boat laughing as they watched our antics. Back on the boat quite away from the shore just about everyone on the boat, except the crew, started to feel sea-sick. The malady came upon us and swept from bow to stern all wanted to be on the shore as there was not a pair of 'sea-legs' among us. Back on land everyone gathered around the hotel swimming pool the adversity had united us although we were all strangers, conversations began we learned of the adventures of all the other couples and they listened to ours. The sunsets in a moment on the equator so we went back to our room to shower and dress for dinner. He was so gorgeous then and now we are both so old, every time I look at him I still see him, my man bobbing around in that blue sea. Neither of us can move easily now we will be eight six years old this year, he in October and me in November. I know we would both go back in an instant, if only we could, to that beach and the Indian Ocean where I made these photographs forty years ago.

All the Way to Berlin

It was a kind green-grey uniform and the shape of the hat that made me look as the border guard put his head through my car window and asked for my passport. He wanted money as well, no it was not a bribe, it was the cost of driving a posh western car along the autobahn from Helmstedt through East Germany to Berlin. The passport and everyone else's passports were hooked up by some conveyor belt contraption and into a pillbox where sat another solider checking and stamping with his rubber stamp. It was always adrenalin-y this experience standing on the border of west and east in the middle of the cold war. Yet another guard and his dog was sniffing around the car checking for whatever it was looking for. There were lookout towers which held guards who trained machine guns across the Zoll posts and a great stone plinth with a tank pointing threateningly towards the west. Streams of cars going both west and east impatiently waited their turns. Then the officer turned again to me with a huge smile and said, using my full name, "Ah you have one of those new car telephones. I require another thirty-five marks to allow you to drive it to Berlin." I smiled and said "but will not work here." He smiled back and said "I know! Do you need change? Oh it will cost you the same on your return journey. You could remove the aerial of course, maybe no one notices, but I know they will, it's our job. Oh your passport and remember fifty kilometres per hour all the way to Berlin." I started the engine and drifted off behind the stream of cars I could do nothing but follow. Through my rear view mirror I saw the East German stick his head in the window of the car which was following me. Then it was East Germany and their funny little Trabant cars all the way to Berlin.

If Only

It was the count down to disaster. Sandra was looking at her watch. All those years ago you came to this restaurant, in your memory it was better back then. The place used to be full of people and it was a novelty, pay a fixed price and eat what you can, I do not know if they were the first to come up with that idea, they were certainly the first I knew. The food was so good and such a choice. That was then, this was now. Of course you did not know as she looked down bored and wishing she was elsewhere. You the unsuspecting fool. Of course you were not unsuspecting you had started the ball rolling a few weeks ago. After all there was nothing in it, it was just a meeting, three old friends who had not seen each other for, how many years was it ago? A life time and more. If only Sandra had looked up from her watch and said: "Whatever you are planning it is the scheme of a real fool and you should abandon the whole idea here and now. Think of what is a stake."

Sandra glanced along the table at the other guests of this party then gave her husband the look, if he had seen it, it would have cut through him and told him that she had had enough and it was time to leave but Brian was chatting with the woman he was sitting next to. Sandra was a little bit jealous. The woman what was she up to? Thought Sandra. Then two of the children started laughing, they were so loud that their mother gave them a look which said: "We are in a very nice restaurant, that is enough!" The children laughed a bit more but then they paused. Sandra coughed and stood. She tapped Brian on the shoulder and said: "Good night everyone. Nice to see you all after such along time." If I had only taken her lead, if I had only just walked away. Life is full of 'if onlys'.

Disappointments

I can tell you I have had some disappointments in my life. You have had a load too I'll bet that is absolutely for certain. What I first saw this feature on my computer I thought oh that is good. It is better than the screen savers from *Windows 95,* gosh that was before my younger daughter was born and she is already more than a quarter of a century old! The pictures in the computer cycle through on the screen, I clicked the *properties* tab it seems I have loaded 22000 photographs in there. I have two screens and so two pictures change every minute or so. In the beginning I was astounded by the number of photographs I did not remember seeing before, even now I glance and I see something new. Of course if I am working, writing something the pictures are covered with my work, so the pictures wind through without me seeing. It has been this way for a good number of years now so even with 22000 photos I am getting a little bored of the same images. Actually I am somewhat disgruntled as many remind me of the disappointments I have had to endure. Then I shake my head because I know it is my choice to think that way. There was a picture of one of my children riding one of our horses. So proud, in control and so free, off up into the forest, away into the snow, not a care in the world. That is how I wanted it to be for my children. Unburdened by the constant drone that it is possible to hear on most lips these days "be careful; it could be dangerous; you might hurt yourself; I hope they will be alright". I am not saying throw caution to the wind but sometimes it is stifling. I was speaking with a policeman. I said, innocently, that it was wonderful to live in such a wonderful place where the children were free to ride off on their horses. He looked at me and said "It only takes one bad person to make the forest unsafe!" Oh how I wish I had not said a word! My intention had been to praise the law and the order in the country and to hint that I was thankful for the work he and his colleagues did to keep up all safe. The people who have been the most disappointing in my life have not often been strangers, they have been people I have known well. I suppose it is obvious really those who are the closest know your weak spots then they can become the most disappointing thing you remember.

Hirple

"Are you squeamish?" The doctor asked as she greeted me from my long hirple (limp) from the x-ray department back to her office. She looked excited 'at last a patient who really needs my attention' was painted in her eyes. I suppose when you are a doctor you see many things which are uncomfortable and on occasion something you know is going to put your wit to the test to cure. Maybe police officers have the same thing when a murder turns up on their patch, despite what television dramas would have you believe murders are not that common some police people must go a whole career without investigating one. So I went into her room and with difficulty eased myself on to the chair. I had had a hip x-ray one year before she pointed to the relevant area on her computer screen she said:

"This is your left leg the top of this bone, the femur has a ball which fits in to a socket which is apart of your hip bone. You can see a darker line between these bones, this is how it should look. Now if we look at your right leg you can see that the dark line is thinner on the right of the line. This is an indication of Osteoarthritis. One year ago we would have understood if you were experiencing discomfort but the situation was not so advanced as to warrant surgical intervention. Now I will show you the x-ray you have just had taken. As you can see the left leg is still good. However, the right leg has no dark line between the bones at all now, You have bone grinding on bone and I would hazard a guess that by now your right leg is considerably shorter than the left and that is why you are limping and why everything is so painful.

Bryony

"I am telling you Philip be cautious. I know you are head over heals and in love right now, if it all works out for you I will be pleased but take a deep breath and really think on it before you ask her to marry you. I know you do not want to hear me say these things. I am saying them because so many people failed to say to me what they were thinking before it was all to late. No I am not saying do not marry her I am saying think long term before you do. If I were you I would live with her first and see if that works out. You really do not know anyone before you live with them. She will blow your mind as she is completely opposite to you and you will spend most of your life picking up after her because you are neat and tidy and she is not!"....... I did not hear from Philip for a few months after that conversation, I was worried that my outburst had caused me to loose a dear friend. Then his call came and he said: "James I was really very upset by our last conversation, I did not like being told to my face that I should be cautious about asking Bryony to marry me. That is why I have not been in touch. I am sorry and I have missed you, your friendship has always been something very special in my life. Anyway Bryony did move in with me. It was alright for a couple of weeks, yes you were right chaos, clothes everywhere, the word tidy is not apart of her character. Then there were all these things in the kitchen, she insisted that I should follow the diet she preferred. Green teas and anchovies on pizza. I said to her look you like those things so you eat them, I do not like them so there is more for you I will eat this. Well that did not go down well. Before that we had really only eaten in restaurants so she chose what she wanted and I had what I liked. That was not the worst of it. James I have worked hard these years and each of the things I own I had to earn the money for. That is what really did if for me with Bryony. I had to go away on business for a week. When I returned she had completely remodelled the apartment. Completely! The furniture was all new and the colour scheme. I really do not know how she found decorators or got the furniture changed with no reference to me at all. The worst of it was when I arrived home there was a cardboard box by the door it had 'For *MacMillians* Hospice Shop' scored on it in black magic marker. I looked inside and there was the complete dinner service, plates, cups, glasses and cutlery each piece wrapped in newspaper. That collection took me several years to accumulate and I really loved having friends to dinner and laying it out on the table, well you know it you have eaten off those plates many times. It was strange I did not put my key in the lock to open the door I rang the doorbell, I was in such a shock, then of course I saw the apartment for the first time in it's fresh new décor. James it did not suit me one little bit. You know I am a mild mannered person but I lost my temper at all of this and I have not seen Bryony since.

25 Years of Blanket

It really was not my ambition to become an employee in this place. I was free lance. I popped in two or three times a year and did what I was asked to and disappeared again. Although I had to be on the ball every visit everywhere I went, I was happy with the pressure. If you work in a place every day and you have an 'off day' it gets swallowed up in all the other days and is not noticeable. As I was only there once in a while there were no days to swallow any bad performance!.... Disaster had come to my door and these guys had thrown me a life line I was not sure how it could all work but if you are on a raft in the Pacific ocean and an oil tanker throws you a line you cling on for there is little choice you do not criticise them for global warming. I jumped into this with all my heart and I really tried to make a go of it. It seemed to me that from adversity I had ceased an opportunity to try something new. So I worked and I worked but realised as freelance I was *Mr Super Person*. This status had melted and that a completely new set of skills were required to work every day in the same spot rather than work in that spot a couple of times a year. I lacked the training and it took me time to realise the problem ... I was great freelance mediocre full time. Still somehow or another we got from September until the following July, it was the end of the term and I was still alive. There was a big end of year celebration with music and thank you-s and presents for those moving on. That is how I came by this blanket. Traditional Scottish wool tartan. I was *no* very satisfied with that year of my life and when they gave me the present it felt like they had found something at the back of the cupboard that *would do....* It was cold last night and although that year was hard this blanket is still doing it's job a quarter of a century later. I have wondered at times if any of the things I tried to teach that crowd had been learned by any of them. All those gems all those pearls of wisdom. I will never know if they rejected or accepted or if the ideas seeped into their minds and became theirs totally disassociated with anything they remember of me. How could I think that they remembered me anyway? If they did it may not have been in a positive way. I did see one of them on the television when Queen Elizabeth was buried, yes a Princess, she asked for my autograph once. I noted too that several Olympic gold medallists had attended those lectures of mine. I could not claim the glory of course but there is a part of me that hopes that some of the things I tried to put across helped them to success. Maybe others from that elite group had success in fields which go unpublicised and I know I am really going beyond myself to think that some of these students may have by now had children and sage like they have imparted the wisdom I had hoped to give to them. It probably does not matter anyway. I am old now I can hardly move, I did my best for them and in doing so kept a roof over the heads of my family and also I got this blanket. I am going to put it around my shoulders right now, it will keep out the autumn chill even if it were something they found in the back of the cupboard, it is still working today twenty five years on.

Washing Machines

I was a single parent with an unusual occupation. My child was two when his father left. There was no money and so I just got on taking the child with me to all the different places I had to work. He was really great. I used to lay out a great pile of toys to keep him amused on one side of the room and then deal with my clients on the other. My clients were very understanding, well most of them of course there was the odd horrible one who made a fuss. My kid and I travelled far and wide, country to country. There were plenty of challenges, getting the washing done in Germany was one of those. I found a laundry one day but I did not understand the words *trocken* and *bügeln, dry and iron.* So after work we went to pick up the washing but it was wet and I had no hope of drying it in the February cold. We found an hotel and I put the clothes on the radiator only to find some evil baddy had put chewing gum on the back side of the radiator and it attached to the clean clothes! A few days later we were in Bavaria, there were mountains and the *Four Track* car that I drove looked really filthy. I needed to buy petrol and the garage had a carwash so I paid for the super wash and dry. The carwash was drive in, reverse out. The machine started to whirl, spray and scrub but then the horizontal scrubbing roller got caught under the spare wheel which was attached to the rear door of the car. It kept on rolling and foam built up and up my little one got quite nervous, as did I, we were now unable to see through the windscreen due to the excess foam which had engulfed the car. The roller kept turning relentlessly. I sounded the car horn and no one came. I worked myself in to quite a lather. I could not get out of the car without being soaked and covered in bubbles and I thought that maybe the noise of the brushes and the gushing of the water was drowning out the sound of the horn. It was nearly twenty minutes before the next person who wanted to use the car wash arrived and fortunately for us he raised the alarm and got assistance. The saga continued for over an hour as the roller brush had to be unbolted and they could not unbolt it without stopping it. The switch to turn of the electricity was actually right in front of me but I did not realise. So they had to switch off the main supply to the whole garage. It was only when we realised that the roller brush had stopped and the sound of the water gushing had ceased that we thought there was help to release us from this watery situation. Neither my son or I have been keen on carwashes since even if they are the drive through variety. We have been really happy to see the growth of the hand car wash business. He is all grown up now but will never drive into a car wash.

The Singalong

It was 11:15 on that Saturday night it was my third professional gig. The first was a disaster, the second I got away with and the gig I had just finished was the best of this small bunch. It was all still new. I had been singing as an amateur since I was 5 years old. Now I was in a real market place selling my services as a singer and I was so out of my depth I was drowning. The night of the first gig a rough looking man came over to my little stage in the corner of the rough pub, by the dart board, they often put the singer by the dart board, the man was very big, he had a pint jug of beer in his hand and he roared at me: "Can you sing 'Rock a Round the Clock' mate?" my nervous response was "No!" He then shouted "Why don't you Fxxx off then?" So there I was the third gig of my career, I had to make this work I had resigned from my 'real job'. At the end of the two and a half hours a man wandered over to me. He had a kindly face and a wide parting in the hair of his head. His expression said he had heard it all before. I thought he might be going to tell me that I was a waste of space instead he said: "Look son I can see you are young and it is obvious you have not done this sort of gig much before. Look you have a nice face, your hair is a bit long, your are dressed well, your amplifier works well, you play the guitar well and you have a great voice. The problem is you sing all the wrong songs." So I got out my note book and pen and I wrote down a list of songs that he said I should sing in the pubs of that time. I knew none of them! I can tell you I learned them all of them and more. Now I have come to then end of my career and I still cherish that list. Look here it is. You see I was a teenager then and he was probably twenty years older than me back then. Guess what it has been the same all these years most of my audience has been ten or twenty years my senior and so these past years I found those people they are in Care Homes and Sheltered Housing places and they have always been happy to listen to the songs that I wrote down on that list 47 years ago. You know with that list and all that flowed from it, I did gigs in twenty five countries, I married and divorced three women. I raised four children. Sometimes there was not quite enough money but we had new cars and the children had horses and there was always good food and clothes and a roof to kept all of us warm and dry. I met wonderful people and was accepted into situations that few will ever have the opportunity to experience. I wish I have been able to keep a record of that man's name and address but it was not something I thought of at the time and I was never invited back to that pub so I never met him again. Oh for a time machine so I could find him and show him what his kindness did for me. Now in the modern era I had a text message from a young singer, she complained that the gig she did in a care home had not gone so well. I replied: 'It is probably the choice of songs at the beginning of your show. You have fixed on one show and what you will find is that some older people can be sensitive about their age. I said you might find people as young as me(!) with dementia or a physical infirmity in your show they do not feel old and do not want you to think they are old. So get together a bunch of songs from the years when they were teenagers start the show with those and then the older songs as you progress through the show.'

The Key Ring

I have great difficulty walking, I really need some replacement parts. If I can ever get to the top of the list down at the hospital I know I could be running the marathon once more (that is a fib—I have never run in a marathon). The bother is without my trusty stick I really can go only a short distance at a very slow pace. Even with the stick I cannot move that quickly. I am not complaining (yes I am) I just wish I could move like I used to. Still the tablets do ease the pains. The worst of it is in bed at night, ok I will stop going on. Things are what they are. I was in the hospital for another x-ray and the first person I saw was in a wheelchair the poor fellow had no legs at all! The next person I saw had only one leg. So in stark reality I am very fortunate I have two and one of them is functioning pretty well. I was thinking about the stick. I really use it to take some of the weight off the joints in my leg by using the muscle in my arm. Before the stick comes in contact with the ground my shoulder, the elbow and the wrist are all involved. I thought I would buy a crutch and then the weight would be supported directly by my armpit straight down to the ground. So I spent ages on the internet looking for one crutch, they normally come in pairs, the price had to be affordable. There was a waiting time of three weeks on the one I purchased. I was expecting no other parcels so when I had a text message from a delivery company saying my package would be delivered early I was so excited. The delivery person handed me a small package, certainly to small to be a crutch, I had no idea what it was. There was no senders address, I opened the packet and there was a key ring which professed 'I LOVE YOU'! I could not return it and I continued to wait for the crutch. Last evening I checked the website for my order and written there was it had been delivered on the day I received the key ring! I wrote to them of my confusion. They replied 'Oh dear we made a mistake, we sent your crutch to someone who ordered a key ring!' Well I did think 'what company handles both key rings and crutches?' Then I realised that there could be someone out in the wilds somewhere who is using my crutch as a key ring!

The Book Stop

I went to the *book stop* last Friday. I sat under the shelter on that uncomfortable seat of metal bars. The shelter has been graffiti-ed expect the end where the *Banxi* picture is. That appeared overnight, some say it is a miracle, the very next day the council put a frame around it with toughened glass and twenty-four hour CCTV. Now that they can watch this remote stop all the time you might think they would give it a lick of paint and cover the horrible infantile pictures of penises but the council has not bothered. When I first started using this *book stop* I was still in primary school now I sit clutching my free book pass waiting for the right book to come along. Of course it takes a lot longer these days because it is not just books that go past here. No, there are endless magazines, CDs, DVDs, BlueRay. There are even computer programmes on USB sticks and no end of computer games. Since last summer we even get downloads passing by this *book stop*. You should see the books that pass everything from *Mills and Boon* romance to sophisticated text books on all manner of subjects some professors of universities would find heavy going. All the classics come by too and endless streams of literature from every country and in many different languages. *Mau's Little Red Book* of Chinese communism whizzed by a few minutes ago, *Andrew Morton's* tome on *Monica Lewinsky* (who would keep a dirty dress in the closet for so long? Monika obviously!). Then there was *Computing for Dummies* and an atlas of the moon. Last Friday I had to come out in my thick jacket and boots there was a mean east wind, I was so pleased I bought my flask of hot tea along. I sat waiting for one particular volume to turn up. I had to sit there from a quarter past nine until twelve minutes past one! Then I looked at my watch and realised I had the wrong Friday! Would you believe it? I could hardly believe it myself of all the Fridays I have sat through over these past twelve months the Friday I needed was still in the future. No wonder the book I was looking for did no show up it had yet to be published. I will tell you this for nothing, you need to be careful how you pick your Friday's they can be illusive as a Monday or even a Wednesday if you fail to get a grip. You must also guard against the fact that they can be inconclusive, damp, sullen as well as being bright, joyous and glorious. I have been around Fridays all my life and some have been filled with so much sun it would have been difficult to push more in. This *book stop* is my favourite. I have tried others but for all they may look, smell and feel similar I always know when I am at my *book stop* this is the one that suits me, the books from here go further, they go everywhere and some say even further than that. I am cheeky to call it mine, it is a public amenity which any individual can take advantage off, I wish more people would use it. I am far from the only person who does and I do get jealous if I pass and see someone else sitting in my spot. It is opposite the park so you get a lot of children's literature here too. A classic just went by that my weans adored back in the day *Spot the Dog*. I am awfully sorry I will have to leave you hanging, mine has just arrived and the driver is impatient and says he will only accept the exact change, I have waved my book pass at him, everything is fine.

Cloud Burst Situation

There were some people staying, friends of his wife, he did not much care for them so he found some extra work to do and kept away for most of their visit. On the Friday evening he finished his shift at ten o'clock by the time he arrived home it was eleven. It had just started to rain has he put the car on the drive way. In the house he made himself a sandwich and a cup of hot chocolate. His wife's friends bought newspapers, Graham never did. So as he sat in the living room by the gas fire enjoying his sandwich he picked up a copy of the Daily, oh my he thought: 'this is the trash they fill their heads with no wonder I cannot abide them.' He thumbed through the pages of salacious rubbish and could not imagine paying for such garbage. Then he became aware of the sound of water. He could not quite make out from where. Maybe one of the guests was taking a midnight bath. He put down the paper and walked into the hall the water noises where coming from the other side of the front door. This is where he made a big mistake. He turned the key and unlocked the door and he pulled it open. A great tidal wave of brown water gushed into the house and before he knew what had happened he was knee deep in flood. It took a while before the person on the council emergency desk answered the telephone, it took a further wait before Graham was speaking with the man who was in charge of drains. The poor fellow had been disturbed from his slumber and his annoyance was as a watermark in the tones that came from his mouth and burnt into Grahams ear. Graham said: "I am sorry but I am not sure what you just said would you mind repeating it for me?" The drains man said: "I cannot come out at the moment sir there is a cloud burst situation." "I am sorry what do you mean?" Graham replied. "It is a CLOUD BURST SITUATION SIR it is raining!" "Yes I know. So you are telling me that you cannot come out and help me until the rain stops. Is that right?" The drains man said: "That is correct we can only come outside a CLOUD BURST SITUATION to a situation when it is dry." Graham let out a chuckle and then said in exasperation: "The road on which I live is just around the corner from the main road into the town. There is a shop opposite and more shops around the corner. My house is in a hollow but the water level has spread across the road to the hardware store and to the garage car repair shop and it will not be long before my neighbours basement is full of water. The water is coming up through a drain in the middle of the street." The drains man said "I do sympathise sir." Graham put the phone down without saying more. On the floor above his wife and guests were still in deep sleep, he was thigh deep in sewage water.

Then there was a knocking on the door and a short man with a moustache and a yellow sou'wester hat, yellow raincoat and Wellingtons announced that he was the drains man and as the cloud burst situation had finished he would be able to offer assistance. Before long he had a set of drainage rods linked up and was busy pushing them down into the manhole. It did no good for all his ramming could never be enough. It was getting light when a gang of men turned up with pneumatic drills and a digger. Another truck came and sucked up a lot of the water. They discovered that the drainage pipes had been crushed. This small street was not meant to take the weight of double-decker buses trundling upon them day after day. It turned out that the manager of the bus garage, which was in another street half a mile away had given drivers the instruction to use Graham's road. The manager had not consulted with the council about the change and the consequences were very expensive as the road had not been designed to take such a lot of weight each day.

Staying Awake

Sleeping was difficult for Granny. Her husband was a man who had a very loud snore. He could not help it, and he needed his sleep for he worked so hard in the factory, five and a half days every week. She used wax earplugs to try to shield her eardrums from the vibration and the doctor supplied a stream of sleeping tablets, which seemed to Granny to get weaker with every new batch. At six each morning the 'Teasmaid' would fizz and gurgle into a steaming stream of boiling water, only a few inches from Granny's head, which was covered by her sheet, hemming the night beneath it and protecting her from the day. Granddad would rise with the final gurgle and take the tea pot to the tray, near the foot of the bed, which he had prepared the night before. He would put milk from a small jug into two cups, and pour the brewed tea on top of the milk. Then he would put granny's cup on the very small space beside the 'Teasmaid' on the table beside the bed. Granny pretended to doze, still hidden, corpse like, beneath the white sheet.

Granddad would then go to the bathroom and rattle and gurgle, not unlike the 'Teasmaid' and during this time another sound would travel up the stair from the front door below, the newspaper delivery boy would push the newspapers through the letter-box. Shortly after the post-man would push the days letters into the letterbox as well, causing the newspapers to thud to the doormat below followed by the cascade of envelopes. The stairs would creak as Granddad descended to get himself his breakfast. The water in the kitchen sink swished and then the crockery chinked as he returned is bowl and cup, clean and dry, into the cupboard, and the sound of the air being pressurised, as the cupboard door swung shut, and the click of the latch as Granddad made the door fast. He would then bring the newspapers and the un-opened letters up the stairs and place them on to his side of the double bed. Granny would then remove the sheet from her face and Granddad would lean over and kiss his wife, gently on the forehead. He would say "See you at lunch time." Then off he would go, and from the front door below a cold draft would rush up the staircase and force it's way into the bedroom, as he closed it behind him. After lunch Granny would try to snatch a few moments of sleep, she would sit in her armchair and cover her eyes with a black leather glove. She never really slept in the afternoon. People will tell you that sleep is when the body and mind recuperate. 'There is nothing like a good night's sleep', people say. The mattress makers are always quick to point out that their wonderful support system will hold your body in cool perfect posture so you can wake refreshed and truly alive each day. I find sleep more of a challenge these days. It is a kind of fruit machine. Put a pound in the slot, pull the handle and hope for three pineapples. Many nights is two bells and a cherry. Sometimes I sleep in the middle of a Technicolor action movie, so vivid it is as real life, then I wake and have forgotten the dreams plot and the story before I have kicked off the duvet. Many times I wake and I cannot breath through my nose and that makes me feel as if I will suffocate, so I give up and get up, to early. On occasion I roll over at see a sliver of light through the shutters and the barely visible hands of the clock are at ten and I feel great for I had enough sleep. Today it was six thirty and so I wrote you this, for later today I will probably be typing away, my eyelids will droop and I will fall asleep in this chair for an hour or so because I cannot stay awake.

New Hip

My friend chapped the door 06:30 bang on time. I hirpled (limped) to the dustbin on my walking stick in the dark and deposited a bag of rubbish. We drove twenty miles then I dragged my limping leg along the hospital corridors to the ward. A smiling nurse showed me to my chair. There were questions, blood taking and then a pleasantly spoken woman arrived she was the consultant anaesthetist. The room filled with others maybe ten all with the expectation of knee and hip repair. The consultant explained her role and moments later I was in a room with eight bed-stations. I was told to put on a hospital gown. I had no sooner done that when a nurse provided a small beaker containing a cocktail tablets designed to start putting me to sleep. The idea was to inject some liquid into my spine to make my legs go to sleep and to sedate me so I was unaware of the operation I was about to be given. This is different from having a 'General Anaesthetic'. They said it would make my recovery quicker. I was also offered the choice of having the operation without sedation so I would be a wake and aware during the procedure; call me chicken but I did not fancy that!

I remember the doctor pressing a metal rod on my skin, she asked me if I could feel how cold it was. She started off by my knee and I did not feel it until it reached my tummy. After droning on to these attentive doctors until I had bored them with my chatter I was in a deep sleep unaware of anything until a nurse was rousing me from slumber. I could see the clock it was almost midday the nurse said: "It is time for lunch!" I asked if I had the new hip and her reply was: "Yes." My misplaced apprehension was dissipated. My worries about the 'pain', 'will it go well', 'what would it feel like to have non-organic parts inside me' were vanquished. The nurse said: "Tell me if you have any pain it is easier to keep pain under control rather than to try to get it under control." During the afternoon several people enquired as to how I was feeling. The physiotherapist came before the anaesthetic had worn off so he said he would be back in the morn. 16:00 I could wriggle my toes and feel an itch on my right calf. The staff were kind efficient and supremely professional. During their twelve hour shifts they scuttled about in unrelenting circles attending to every need and requirement. The night staff worked their shift with equal vigour. Unbelievably mid-afternoon the following day I had been instructed in the use of crutches, been given a series of exercises, practised walking up and down the corridor and I climbed a short flight of stairs. A nurse showed me how to inject myself with medicine that prevents blood clots. I was given a large bag of medication including a sharps container and the dressings and stitch cutter for the nurse at my GP surgery for the change of dressing a week later and for the stitch removal a week after that. There were instructions to make appointments with the nurse and a discharge letter. Telephone numbers and warnings to call should anything be amiss. Not only were the staff excellent whilst I was at the hospital the following morning a nurse from the ward called to check I was alright. In 35 hours from leaving home to returning I had a new hip and was without pain for the first time since I cannot remember. I could move using the crutches for safety my new hip bore the weight with no bother. Wednesday morning I went into hospital looking for a new hip Thursday afternoon I came home as a revitalised person and a desire to out live the 30 year life expectancy of that hip.

The Machine that Goes Ping

I watched it was quite the background sound was the breeze, the hum of insects and birds calling. There in the shade from the bright summer sun under that deep blue sky, that is only available in July and early August in this place. There was no stress, no one shouting, no one giving spurious advice. None was required. The fact that this was the first time she had done this did not matter either as nature will do what nature does, regardless of human-kind's clod-hopping, over sized, rubber boots. So it came to pass that on that twenty-first day of July five tiny fur covered kittens were born. There was no machine going ping or monitoring of heartbeats or epidural. Look about the world, when I was at school the earth was home to fewer than three billion people. As I write these words there are close to eight billion people, many of them born with no aid from medical authorities. No machine that goes ping (if you are trying to remember where the *machine that goes ping* came from the *Monty Python* team their film *The Meaning of Life*). If you have been paying attention to your '*Good Books* reading list' you will know that the meaning of life is actually 'forty-two', as forty-two is the natural number that follows forty-one and precedes forty-three. The great late *Douglas Adams* worked that out years ago. (*Hitchhiker's Guide to the Galaxy*). There is need to panic now, for more people make more and more people, and more, and more people demand more, and more stuff. What are you giving up? Yes, I thought so. I really do not wish to stop doing, eating, travelling or using the machines that go ping. I write in this in a small haven which even in the world storms of recent times has kept me from too much harm. There are people who will advertise the idea that we can 'go-back' to the way things were done before. Sure there will be some disciples who follow such a path, good luck to them all. The truth is though life is a forward progression. *Paul Simon* has a line in one of his songs *The Teacher, because it's easier to learn than unlearn, because we passed the point of no return*. That is true; think of some skill you have developed, pottery, needle work, playing piano, if you have some mastery of any such skill you cannot go back to the day you first sat at the piano and repeat the way you approached it on that day, your brain will not allow it. There is another *Paul Simon* lyric *The planet groans every time it registers another birth*. For all humankind's over-sized rubber boots it is astonishing just what our species can do. Although we do not always get it right, some may be left out, some left behind, it is simply science fiction come to life that from *Valdimir Putin* to a homeless person, collecting coins on the street corner in *Ayr*, billions of people have a mobile phone to hand twenty-four hours a day. Despite the world being totally awash with human kind, there are still not enough people to do all that needs to be done! So the health-service experiments with robots to care for the elderly and robots pick goods from the shelves in huge warehouses and computers arrange the transport of the exact item you ordered straight to your door. I sat next to a woman a few years ago on an aeroplane and as we took off into the sky I said to her: "We live in a magical world don't we?" She looked at me and asked me: "What do you mean by that statement?" I asked her: "Do you not think that it is it magical that we can fly?" Scotland's clinical director during the Covd Pandemic was *Jason Leitch*. He said that the idea of people having a test, that they can perform in their own home to see if they have a deadly virus was the stuff of science fiction. He was right. I pin my hope for the future on the brilliant minds, ingenuity and the amazing cleverness of so many of my fellow human's. I say thank you as my first child's life was saved, at it's beginning, by a *machine that went ping*. I am ever grateful that that little boy has grown into a fine man, just one of the eight billion or so of us clinging to this precious little rock, among trillions of other rocks in this universe of ours.

Justice?

The government message was to go and get a better job one that pays more and stop sponging of the state. Helen had heard it all before. It is alright for them all those politicians they have money enough. All the bankers and business owners maybe if they had a little bit less there would be a bit more for the poor. Helen looked at the mould on the wall which stretched up to the ceiling by the window of what was laughingly called a kitchen. She saw the advertising for dream kitchens but for all the sixty and more hours she put into her two jobs each week there was not even enough money left to buy a tin of paint to cover that awful black cloud of mould. Besides the manger of this social housing could easily evict her if she were to try and improve the damp situation. She had given up spraying the mould killer and wiping it away. She just felt lucky that she was better off than her neighbour whose flat was flooded by a burst pipe in the ceiling of his bathroom. Helen had given up a whole days wages today, not only that she had had to spend precious food money on a bus fare to the interview.

The human resources woman who had conducted the interview was very nice. Then just as Helen thought she was getting somewhere the HR lady said: "Yes you are simply the best qualified person I have seen for this post and in other circumstances I would be happy to recommend you for the position but I have done my due diligence and it unearthed your conviction. Helen froze it took her a moment to compose herself but she had practiced this scenario in her head before the interview. It was the one flaw that all her previous interviewers had picked up on. She knew it would come up again. She looked straight into the eyes of the human resources woman and said: "I got that conviction not because I did any wrong. The company I worked for went bust because the owners of the company committed fraud I was the accountant doing their books using the figures and information that they gave to me. I was at all times totally honest and I kept the books correctly using the information that I was given I had no control of the information that was given to me but the company directors told the police I was involved in their criminality and I could not make the court understand that I was not. The conviction is sixteen years old it has nothing to do with what I was or what I am or what I could do for your company. I was told that the conviction would be 'spent' after a few years and that then I would be free of it as if the time I served in prison was not enough punishment for something I had not done. The government says I should get a better job. I would like a better job and you would like to employ me but you will not and all because of something that I did not do sixteen years ago. I have heard the pious idiots chanting 'do the crime – do the time' they have no idea every sentence in this two bit country is a life sentence. I was in prison with a young girl who was accused of shop lifting, her toddler had dropped a bag of sweets into her bag and she had not a clue until she had paid for the rest of her shopping and had walked out of the store. The security man stopped her then there were police who tasered her and she has not seen her child since." Helen stood up, walked to the door and said: "Justice, it does not exist."

Cnut

There was once a King by the name of Cnut who said to his people words to this effect: "I am not a God. If I stood by the ocean and told the waves to go back they would take no heed of my demand." That was misreported leaving suggestions in the minds of people to this day that Cnut (Knut-Canute-Canewt) was able to tell the sea to go back and it would. If he chose the moment that the tide turned he could have made it look as if had such power but people would have seen through that gag quite quickly, the collective memory loves magic in a story and the falsehoods linger far beyond the sell by date. Cnut, so *they* say (who are *they* exactly?), was a King of Denmark and made a pretty good job of building himself an Empire. Although in 1016 when *they* say he became King of England there was not much in the way of keeping records or even communicating who was or was not in charge. A point illustrated wonderfully in a film made by *Monty Python* team in *The Meaning of Life*. There is a scene where a peasant, in time of the Plague, is speaking with the Body Collector. They see the King and the peasant asks: 'Who was that?' The Body Collector replies: "He must be a King. He's the only one who isn't covered in….." How did anyone know who was king back in the day? The King gave responsibility to Lords and the like and their henchmen put the word about.

Cnut came all the way to Scotland a long trip back then well before the M6 and M74. He got all the way to Sterling as that was the place where the mighty Firth of Forth could be crossed and allow entrance to the 'Highlands of Scotland' - Alba. Cnut wanted to include Scotland in his Empire, Why would he not? Such a beautiful country. However at Sterling Bridge he met with Malcolm II of Scotland and he was known for being a 'Strong Man' he killed off anyone who could have taken the throne or threaten his position as Scotland's High King. They called him *Malcolm the Destroyer*. The area around the old Sterling Bridge, now Causewayhead, was a water logged bog with one mile of causeway. Malcolm could easily defend this and thus obstruct Cnut's entry into Alba and the Highlands. So Cnut and Malcolm negotiated, Cnut gave up on the idea of taking Alba under is wing and Malcolm crossed his fingers and said: "OK Cnut you be 'Over Lord' of the Southern part of Scotland but I am still the High King of all Scotland!' Malcolm also paid Cnut *fealty and tribute of one serf, one cow, one horse and one bushel of meal for Lothian, Merse, Teviotdale* and some other 'bits', Malcolm knew he had not the resources to oust Cnut. Now as far as Malcolm was concerned and cow and a horse were not that much of a price to pay after all it was all just words really and Cnut went away and things returned to 'normal'. However, this 'cross fingered agreement' festered over time and six hundred years later English Kings claimed Paramountcy over the WHOLE of Scotland the Lowlands and the Highlands, because of it. History is like the phrase mark on a manuscript of music a note in the first bar can resonate through to the semibreve in the last cadence. Histories stories often are lost but the beat of history lives on long after the event a society may have forgotten the story that started something but they still feel the vibrations. I saw a charming video recently of a wee quine (a little girl) asking her Dad to explain how the Easter Bunny and Jesus rising from the dead with a chocolate egg came about. As many people in Scotland push forwards to REGAIN the Independence of their land maybe revisiting part of the story of how we got to this position might help.

Carpet

'But and Ben' is the name we Scots give to a small house usually two rooms. This house is a wee bit bigger, there is a oxymoron for you wee and bigger all in the same line! Maybe that is what we Scots are, an oxymoron our ancestors started to enlighten the world at much the same time they shackled us to a union with the English so on the one hand we were leading the pack and on the other we were letting our feet be stuck in the concrete mire of English protocol and precedence. After many years of living away in far off countries I returned home. I moved into this wee 'But and Ben' in what was an old mining village. The houses that formed the village were built by the coal board. The village was simply plonked down on a hillside in the wilds of Ayrshire as close to the pits and the open-casts as they could make it saving them as the men could walk to work. There was no history in this place it was purely utilitarian. When the mines closed the houses emptied and they were bulldozed away, a few were left standing and cheaply sold to a few people who wished to remain in the place where they were born. Those folk still hanker for the camaraderie of the days when this island in the hills supported five hundred people. One fellow bought up the land from the coal board speculating that he could build a village to replace that which had been torn down, although he got the land at a low price he has sold very little of it because the only sales features here are solitude and quietness and few young families can live on that, they need it but they need work more

and there is little available around here. My neighbours are a paradox all moan about the closing of the pits and the destruction of the village yet the ones who are left are Tory voters and will have nothing bad said about Margaret Thatcher even though it was her policies that bought an end to what they still pine for. They are simple but good folk and I am lucky to have them as neighbours, however, their lives have always been here anything outside this wee place is foreign. They say that they are worldly wise but none have made it as far as Edinburgh. I had not been here for four days when in the dark, when a hoolie was crashing about outside my back-kitchen door. The rain was lashing and there was my new neighbour trying to raise her Ayrshire speak above the roar of the gale. She informed me that her *dug win awa*, her dog was dead after much suffering and her brother needed help to bury the body. I suggested that I would be happy to do that in the light of the following morning. No it had to be done now, here and now. She was so *pit aboot,* distressed, I put on my Wellingtons and jacket and started to dig a hole in the middle of her lawn. I laid the dug wrapped in a towel in the hole and covered it with earth replacing the sods as best I could. Nothing more was said on this, no thanks was expressed I thought nothing more of it until one fine July morning, four months later I looked out of my windy and saw that there was a mound of earth dug from the middle of my neighbours lawn. I thought 'oh my some has dug that dug up!' I went out to look and thankfully found that the disturbance to the ground was due to a piece of carpet which was obviously been laying in the grass for many years. The grass had grown through the foam back and added to the pattern. I enquired of my neighbour and she told me her brother had been looking for the dead dug's burial place and found the carpet and started to pull it up out of the grass. I asked how it had got there she told me that forty years ago her father had won some money and had bought new carpet the old had been dumped on the grass and left. The grass had grown through it and it had been forgotten. I asked her brother what he was going to do with the carpet he said: "I will pull it up and drag it over to that bit of empty ground over there." He pointed. I said: "No, no, no you told me only the other day how beautiful everything is about here and now you want to dump this rubbish in the middle of it. Leave it I will cut it up and take it to the *cowp* (the dump) It took me the best part of the day and a whole roll of black plastic bags to deal with it all!

Donna Music Queen

I must have been about fifteen when I first saw her band playing live, I thought they were brilliant. I turned up at a lot of their gigs and got to know them. I was asipring to make a living with my singing too and they let me into their group and I roadied for them and watched and learned. Twenty years later I was one of Donna's confidant's but by that time her success was over and although she could not give up the dream it was obvious it would never happen. She still had mighty talent. Her song writing capability was stella class but she had fallen out with those who control the 'big-time' and she spend most of her time in frustration when yet another manager did not call her back. Of course twenty years before she could play the sex card and that worked well in getting her through the door of the mogals, don't give me any guff about *me too*, she knew exactly what she was doing because her ambition was absolutley huge. Things did get a little out of hand one time and so I am godparent to her daughter, a fine woman with children of her own these days. Any time Donna managed to break down some barrier and put her material infront of an executive something went wrong. She never earned a penny from playing her music most of her life she relied on the social and when things were awkward I would fund the gap. She looked down her nose at me. I built a different type of career. I went to holiday camps and I learned my trade from top professionals. On my first summer season I learned all the inflections, all the intensities of my vocal range so that I could command a room of four thousand people and hold their attention. I learned how to hold myself and how to get the best of any punter who had joined one of our silly competitions. Donna never understood those types of skills. She never got past the good tune-great lyric-and sex appeal stage, that only works for a short career. It is close on fifty years that I have earned my income from the entertainment business. I never 'rested' as some of my actor friends, I never did bar-work to fill in time. I diversified into all the skills I could from holiday camps to grand theatres, from slapstick to Shakespeare. I never went short of a gig and I travelled the globe meeting people of all shapes, sizes and colours. Donna said to me once: "The thing is nobody knows who you are, now they know me because my picture was in the *Melody Maker*. I could have said yes twenty years ago but I held back. At the beginning of my career I saw what they were trying to do, tying me down to a role that they thought they could sell. I am so glad I had the sense to see through that or I would have ended up like one of these winning X-Factor stars of the modern era, fine while the record was a hit but dropped when the second did not fly. Donna called me last week in a panic. She reminded me of a professionl flirtation she had had with a then very famous record impresario. I remember clearly the advice I gave at the time: "It is not a good deal, leave it alone." I should have saved my breath of course from her point of view it was acceptance, away back into the big time, so she sold him the publishing rights to a bundle of her then current songs, she did not read the contract properly and that said that all the songs she wrote for the next decade would belong to the publisher. So thirty years later Donna got a letter requesting the money which had been paid as an advance on new work but had never been delivered. It was thousands of pounds, she had thought the money was payment for the songs she handed over at the time. I could not fill that hole and she was now surviving on Universal Credit. Fame was never my aim, I just want to work and bring joy to audiences wherever I could find them, so I bent and fitted myself around as much as I could. Yes I did the radio and the television I put out books and all the rest of it but I used different Nom De Plume and never let anyone tie me up to one role. Looking and the awfulness of the celebrity scene of the modern era it is all but impossible to explain how elated I am that I have nothing to do with them. The aging stars who get their travel show. The less fortunate who get to compare an afternoon quiz show on the telly. Even worse the over fifties life insurance advert. Now we get to the real dregs the voice over for equity release.

Oh but it goes on to the opening of a new supermarket or being wheeled out to be a celebrity on the special afternoon quiz show to raise money for the orphaned donkeys of Tunisia. I cannot advise the young folk looking to join the entertainment scene of today frankly I really do not understand most of it. My advice would be look for work not for fame, avoid fame if you can. Most of the famous entertainers and singers I have known were often unemployed and few made enough money, often those who had one hit song ended up singing it and only it for the rest of their lives. There are few mega stars and few millionaires, if that is what you want go for it. There are plenty of foot soldiers, like me, who have a steady career full of variety, fun and interest. We have the luxury of privacy which is denied to all who go for stardom. I worked in twenty five countries. I raised four children and divorced three spouses. The children had horses and beautiful places in which to grow up. We ate well, dressed well and it was never that far to get back home to them the dogs, the cats and the wonderful mayhem of family life.

Empathy

The mistake, if that is what it was, was to assume that I would always be fine. That I would always have the use of my arms, legs, eyes, mouth, ears, fingers and hands. I have always been protective of myself, whilst not risk averse I would shy away from activities that I felt might damage any bit of me that I might need some day. My left arm became a problem a while ago. The doctor told me that I have trapped the ulna nerve; sadly he provided no comfort nor suggestions for removing the nerve from this wretched trap. So there are many things that I find myself struggling with from doing up buttons to playing the guitar, both of which I am usually rather good at and I miss very much, well not the buttons that is just tiresome. Oh yes I do pick the guitar up and keep trying but it is not right, I cannot do things properly. I am not going to try and pass this off as a major disability in the way that others might be unable to see or walk or whatever, it is merely to point out that I could at one time perform a skill now I cannot. It is frustrating beyond the heavens for me. Travelling here and there doing my work. I liked to meet with the people and bring some comfort and a bit of hope, a little fun into their lives. Everyday I met with people who had been struck down with dementia, strokes, diabetes and other maladies. I used to think how lucky it was not to have to be in a wheelchair or to use a zimmer frame. I could not imagine what it would be like to have to wait for a carer to help me to the bathroom so I could use the toilet. For me so personal and intimate part of my life I shield it from everyone. I had to drive so far for my work and at the end of my day I would climb out of my car the pains in my legs were so uncomfortable but I had suffered those for over twenty years the pains were just a part of me. Many years before a great doctor found a tablet that made those pains vanish. Then after many years another doctor told me I should no longer take them and she gave me another drug of inferior nature, after that it was a back and forth, and argument with each physician I encountered. Then a new doctor told me that he would be happy for me to take the old medicine again, he could not understand why others had been reluctant to let me have it. A very short time later, having swallowed the first of the new batch those pains I had suffered so long were gone. Then I realised that there were other pains, new ones, that were not controlled by the tablet. So over the course of several months it emerged that not only was a new hip required but I needed a new knee as well. Fantastic that I can just write that without blinking after all what could be more natural? The pain at times has stopped me in my tracks. I simply cannot move properly, sometimes I cannot move at all. Getting dressed is monstrous. Then when it comes time for bed It feels like someone is thrusting knitting needles in to my flesh as I lay unable to sleep in the dark. Watching me get into the car must be hilarious, I have to kneel on the drivers seat and then twist my torso and stretch my legs into the foot well. Entering the car in normal fashion is too painful.

The doctor has given pain killers, they do take the edge off that cold, steel like, sharp, ice cold stabbing however there is enough pain remaining so that it cannot be forgotten. I bought a stick over a year ago and will go nowhere without it now, it helps but causes other issues, aching arms and shoulders. Is it that that has caused the trapped nerve? Oh and if I click on Amazon up pop a fine array of new walking sticks, a beauty with a lion's head brass handle, so reasonably priced. Oh and remember to buy some spare ferrules, you never know when one will blow out and leave you slipping across the pavement. Some people have not lived as long as I. I have concerns that I am being greedy wanting more than my fair share of fit and healthy life but in the state I am in at this time I am unable to do many things that I would like to do. Normally I would offer a helping hand to my neighbours currently that is quite impossible. That table turned and now I need them to help me it is very difficult to accept; I have always been a giver, it is so hard to receive and everything takes so long, getting out of bed, hardly being able to put one foot in front of the other to get to the bathroom and grasping for the tablets that will relief that awful sharp pain.

Only a short time ago I saw an opportunity where I could help somebody, I was filled with purpose, I drove to get a stranger from the village, I had to get out of the car to find the lady and when she saw me, hirpling about with my stick she gasped: 'Oh my goodness you are disabled, I would never have put you to such trouble had I known.' So on top of all the pain, the indignity, the lack of being able to pursue things I want to do, suddenly there is a new badge to wear and it says I am not able. If I am not careful that could be how I start to feel useless and before long what is the point of me? I find myself worrying that the bit between my ears will suffer similar impairment as with so many of my contemporaries, and I panic. It maybe that my disability is temporary, maybe I will be lucky, they can fix me up and let me get back on the road. I do not know yet, for now I am trying not to wallow in self-pity. I am trying to do all I can with every moment that I have fighting the frustration and hoping for better times to come. I do appreciate more now just what it is to be disabled and how many people live day to day, year after year, at least I know now of empathy.

Harmony?

"I was just saying that for the ease of getting through this song at the end of term concert, it might be better just to use three chords." Said Marion a little taken a back by the anger expressed by her colleague: "Well I am sorry Marion, I am not of the opinion that making things easy, just to get through something, is the way to go. It is my belief that the people in this country take far, far to many short cuts these days, I think that considerably diminishes our quality of life. We are here to educate the next generation. What kind of example do we set when we say it is ok to simplify this music to the bare bones? After all we are only talking about a couple of chords and there is still time for your guitar group to practice and get that song up to a really good standard. I will not applaud ideas that diminish all the work of this music department." Said the head of music without pausing for breath. "Mr. Baker, I really do not think that the audience will hear the difference, after all Melanie will be the focus of the attention, she will be singing the lyrics and the melody. My 'Spanish Guitar Quartet' are her accompaniment, this will be the first time that they will play before an audience, my fear is that if they fumble over these, quiet complex chord shapes, it will be very awkward for Melanie, and not very impressive to the audience."

"Marion, do you have any idea how hard I have to fight to keep this department of this school open? Everyone sees reading, writing, maths and science as chore subjects that have to be taught, those sorts of subjects have an easy ride Marion. I am afraid Music and its twin Art are very much down the scale of what many people consider necessary school fodder in financially restricted times. Look Marion, some of them want us closed. Many of the rest would be happy to see us cut back to virtually nothing. That is your job, that is my job, on the line! I do not know about you but I have still to work a good few terms before I can claim a pension and at my age finding a replacement for this current employment would, I think, be impossible." "A dilemma then Mr. Baker. Do we make things simple, with a really good chance that Melanie will shine and everything goes smoothly, or do I push these children beyond their current ability, in the hope that they might achieve a level of competence that I feel will take more than the rest of this term to achieve? Either way there is a challenge. We cannot possibly pull the item, Melanie would be very upset and my four guitarists would be upset too, not to mention their Mummies and Daddies." "Look I do understand what you are trying to tell me and I do think you have done a marvellous job with these very young children, to get them to play so well in such a short period of time. It is that I really do have concern about the whole society, every way one turns there is shoddy workmanship, make do and mend, it is as if nobody cares any more. Look at the rubbish that people throw from their car windows. Look at that up there."

"I am sorry Mr. Baker what am I looking at?" "The conduit, for the cables for that television the head had installed on the wall. I mean look at it. A 'professional' tradesman came here; he was in this room from eight thirty on last Tuesday morning. He arrived with his workmate they sat down at my desk, they had tea from their flask and ate a sandwich. They left a ring of tea very close to that pile of music, on my desk and crumbs all over the place. I had to give my lessons that morning, in the gym-hall. There was no prior notification so we all 'froze to death' as it takes over an hour to get that wretched huge space anywhere close to warm. I came back here after my lunch to find the tradesmen shutting the door as they were leaving. There was dust everywhere little curly plastic swirls that had been drilled from the conduit to attach it to the wall. I do hope that there are no sharp edges on the screws which might sink into the wires and cause a short circuit. They should simply have stuck the conduit to the wall it has an adhesive strip on the back they obviously tried and failed to make it stick as the blue tape, which covers the adhesive strip, was just left lying on the cupboard there. There was plaster from where they drilled holes all down the walls and on the floor. Even after they had done all that, they obviously did not use a spirit level and if you look, somehow they actually made it curve in the middle, anymore of a curve and it would be like an unhappy smile! Then look the conduit fails to reach its destination by a centimetre at the television end and two centimetres at the plug end. When you look do you not ask why they did not put the electric cable and the aerial cable within the same conduit? Look how the second conduit is just so un-aligned with the first. It just looks, forgive me Marion, crap." "Yes, I do understand what you are saying. However, in the case of my young musicians it is not a case of 'that will do', obviously in the long term it will not do. So Mr. Baker I will issue them with the challenge, I will use this as an opportunity to show them they could do it the easy way but if they really tried harder they could do it the better way." "Bravo Marion, bravo. I know it will be fine. Young people can be so remarkably good, especially when challenged. I can hardly wait to hear them. Do tell them that Mr. Baker is expecting only the best of performances. Do you know Marion my music teacher, when I began his class when I was eleven years old told me that I would get the performance I expect to get so I had better expect to get the best performance I could. Here we are forty-eight years later and that great teacher is still teaching although he actually past away three years ago." Marion said: "Yes and what some of the people in maths and science forget is that everything that people do requires imagination and we help build children's capacity to imagine with music, art and literature."

Leave

"Just tell me how you can justify that? We made an agreement, I trusted you. You know how important it is to me. Now you have broken the whole thing. Fifteen years. Did you not even think of our daughter? What was going through your mind? If you did this, why would you tell me? I would never, could never have thought this of you. I am so hurt, betrayed. It is not that you are unintelligent you are a Professor in the University, that surely indicates you have a brain and I suppose at times you use it. Your action is the end of us and the end of our lives together. I will take Erika to Edinburgh this afternoon; our flight is just after six o'clock this evening. I have booked a removal firm to come and collect our things, they are all packed. All you have to do is show them where the things are, they will do the rest. They will be coming tomorrow morning at eight, so make sure you are here. I know that will make you late for work but there you go. I just thank heavens I insisted on Erika having her own German passport so there is no problem when we get back home. Yes I know this is our home and it breaks my heart to leave all that we have done together her. No I do not know where we will live, we will go to mein Vater und Mutter im Sternberg, we will stay there until we find somewhere suitable. Yes there are many good things about living here but you have to acknowledge that many things are quiet simply not fit for purpose. Do not get me started about the dirt and the rubbish people throw everywhere. This whole country does so well on the little it's masters allow it, the Government here is progressive and I think they care. If this country were free from colonisation it could be one of the richest countries on the planet. Not while the greedy, incompetent fools in the south enrich themselves to the detriment of the good people here. Anyway a part from the colossal insult you have made towards me, quite frankly, I am sick to death of the constant reminders of *the war*. The snide comments about my *fat country men* and their ability to take over beaches in Spain at the height of summer. Yes that really is the problem, those people, the people who caused all this, the people that have ended our marriage live in the past. The glory days of Empire are over, life is a forward progression and these retrogrades want to turn everything back to how they think it used to be. Well I will tell you how it used to be. In 1967 Harold Wilson and his Government devalued the pound by 14%, they had a huge trade deficit and a weak economy. In the coldest part of the year of 1974 Edward Heath put everyone on a three-day week, everything was in such a mess. Nine years later 1976 Denis Healey had to go to the International Monetary Fund for 2.3 billion pounds, he secured the loan but the United Kingdom finances had then to be run under the supervision of the IMF. You have thrown away opportunity, ruined it for people who want to go where they please, when they please. These stupid, half brain, dumkopf's, lie and cheat and all those little people follow and vote against something they do not understand. Yes it is personal I have given my all to this country for fifteen years; this country has been loyal to me for they voted to stay in. To me that is a vote of confidence in me. This place made me feel at home, these people accepted me, not like some of the racist xenophobes I met when we lived in the other country. I never did tell you the things they said to me, the names they called me. Absolute brutal ignorance of the stupid. If this country is to have a good future the sooner it divorces the south the better. The south is leaching the wealth of this fine place and giving nothing in return. Now it is intent on damaging this country so badly the people here will be even poorer. There is no need for it, if that women had just picked up the phone and called the President and said, I am sorry we made a mistake, we wish to withdraw the letter and wish we had never sent it. The damage that has been done could be repaired. If they go through with this the harm will be enormous. Just how many professors jobs will this lame duck, third world, third-rate country support? Answer me that. Yes I loved you but there is no way I can live with what you say you did. I saw you as my hero; you are the father of our child.

I have respected you and looked up to you for all these years of our marriage and for the time we were courting, so yes you have knocked me off balance. I really cannot believe what you have done. My mind cannot take it in. Things were perfect. You will be contacted by my solicitor with regard our divorce. I will not allow you custody of Erika. I would prefer it if you were to keep away from her. Your poisonous view of politics and total lack of awareness of how I would feel about you doing what you did, are not things I want to be around. Nor do I want them to poison my daughter's mind. It takes years to build things but you and your kind, destroy them for the sake of ignorance and misunderstanding. What you did, I consider to be nothing less than a criminal act, which you will pay for, for the rest of your life. No do not call me back. I never wish to speak with you again. I am leaving I cannot believe you, you of all people voted leave." She took her phone from her ear, she looked at the screen and her fingers erased his details from her contacts.

King Charles III

All things are quite silent, each mortal at rest, when me and my true love lay snug in one nest, when a bold set of ruffians broke into our cave and they forced my dear jewel to plough the salt wave. These lines I have on the album *Living* by *Judy Collins* 1971. *All Things are Quite Silent* is a traditional folk song which speaks of the 'Press-Ganging' of young men, enforced conscription for the Navy. The practice died out by 1835. Young men were ripped from their families, their beds and even their wedding ceremonies. This may not be a conventional view of this subject: I remember hearing the *Today* programme. Broadcaster *Brian Redhead* interviewed *Prince Charles* on the royal train. *Prince Charles* said that if people did not want him to do the job he was doing he would go and do something else. My life has been rich and diverse I have had a full share of disasters and the odd triumph. I did not choose the circumstances of my birth. I would like to argue that all my disasters have been due to other people or extraneous circumstances. I would like to take full credit for any triumph and deny that anyone else had a hand in helping me achieve whatever minor success I think was mine. Of course it would be nonsense to make such claims. I had fortune to come across people who filled me with the feeling that I was a worthy human. I count it the greatest accidents of my birth that I was in no way born into the house of Windsor because whatever I have done in my life, whatever has happened to me it cannot be denied that for good or ill I was in some way or another a part of whatever happened were it good bad or ugly. I inherited no wealth, where I live, the clothes I wear and the food I eat have been obtained through my own industry. I have had times went bills could not be met and times when I have had an excess of funds. I was born and have lived my life in what are known as free countries. I have been able to have my own opinions and been able to voice my pleasure and displeasure. I have been able to mark my cross on ballot papers and although many times the vote has not gone the way I would have wished, at least I did get my chance to make my voice heard. In a world of so many voices I suspect I have lived a life that has been as free as it could possibly have been. I would wish the same for every person born in any part of the world. However looking around one can see that such freedom is unavailable to billions of our fellow humans. People in Afghanistan, China, Russia, Myanmar form an obvious list of those who risk all if they speak out of turn or against those in power. During the change from *Queen Elizabeth I* and *King Charles* as monarchs of Scotland there are many who are against the monarchy's continuation. Many in Scotland would prefer to live in a republic and that cry is also heard in many outposts of the former British Empire. There are many who say that the Royal Family are over privileged so this is to throw a bit of fat on the fire and see if one or two flames ignite. If a judge and jury imprison someone and it is later found that the crime was committed by another compensation has to be paid to the falsely convicted. *Anne, Andrew and Edward, King Charles's* siblings did not choose their parents but they were born into a prison which exists because many in the society support and many wallow in it and wish it to continue—The Monarchy. Every new wean born into that family is incarcerated within the system. The society removes the right of these 'royal' persons to be free, to be able to make their own decisions and live their own lives. If you think they can leave you are mistaken the story of the Duke of Windsor in the 1930's and Prince Harry in the 2020's shows they 'can checkout but never leave' as the lyrics are sung in the song *Hotel California.* In exchange the royals get big houses, cars and servants. Then people moan because there are poor people, homeless people and, and, and…..Many people love the idea of celebrity. They get caught up in the pomp and ceremony and the royals are the ultimate in celebrity. So if you are angry about all the hype and you would prefer a Republic to a Monarchy, remember both ideas do cost money. Maybe though, as I, you will be thankful that your every breath is not documented, your every mistake is not recorded, your every misdemeanour not jumped upon and forever remembered.

My age being not dissimilar to *King Charles* thank my lucky stars that I am not expected to do what he did in his first fortnight as King. I thank my stars I will never have to be monarch. What would happen to the current royals if the doors were flung open and they were 'released' who knows? You may have read *Sue Townsend's* book the *Queen and I.* I wonder what the then *Prince Charles* would have done with his life if he had been able to make other choices when he spoke with *Brian Redhead*. Eventually the people were so fed up the wall around *Berlin* came tumbling down. If you are for a republic then shouting at the king will not bring that about. The change will come because the society at large wishes for something different. For those who support Independence for Scotland it will come about in similar fashion. I would respectfully suggest to those who want a republic, one step at a time. In the meantime thank your god for keeping you out of reach of the press-gangers and be happy you were never dragged away from the life you were planning and forced you to plough the salt wave....As *Prince Charles*, many years ago, Commanded HMS Bronington which later sank, Friday 18 March 2016, in Birkenhead. I read that plans are a foot to re-float and restore this vessel.

Dalrymple

John *Dalrymple* it can be argued is one of the most prominent reasons for the existence of the Scottish National Party. It was he who was instrumental in obtaining enough votes in the Scottish parliament to close it. All of us who hunger for end the Union and want Scotland become an Independent Nation once again, *Dalrymple* was the man that started this. It is worth reminding people that Scotland is the oldest nation in Europe. As with so much history religion is at the core of this story. We still feel the effects of religious battles of the past, today. Forty miles or so up the road from the village of Dalrymple, when *Rangers* and *Celtic* football clubs clash, the matches can be boisterous affairs and the fans after the match sometimes riot. Father passes story to son, mother passes story to daughter and the story breaks free from it's origin and societies forget why something started and why the 'battles' continue today. In 1689 *William of Orange* and his wife *Mary* became the King and the Queen of England and Scotland. Why and how that happened is for another day. The Orange bit is important. You may recall that *Arlene Foster*, of the DUP in Northern Ireland, was in an *Orange Order* march in Fife, the *Orange Order* is a protestant group. *John Dalrymple* was the 'Fluffy Mundell' of his time—The Secretary of State for Scotland--It was upon *John Dalrymple's* orders that the Glencoe Massacre occurred. It was he who sent members of the Campbell Clan to spend time accepting the freely given hospitality of the MacDonald Clan. After the Battle of Killecrankie, you must have heard the

Rabbie Burns song of that name. *Dalrymple*, Secretary of State for Scotland, had a big pile of bribe money from *King William*, to offer to the Clan Chiefs of Scotland, in exchange for them swearing allegiance to William and Mary. Now there is a lot of detail so I will cut to...The Chief of the MacDonald's had failed to pledge allegiance in timely order. So the Campbell's murdered thirty eight of the MacDonald's Clan, men women and children. 13 February 1692. On the orders of *Dalrymple*. Dalrymple, was then promoted and became Earl Stair. The next shameful episode in his life is the one that affects Independence activists the most. You may have heard of the Darien Scheme, Scotland trying to create an Empire for itself, but, say the story tellers, the Scots made stupid blunders, like choosing the wrong goods to trade. Like so many stories that is not the half of it. The Darien Scheme was a huge undertaking for Scotland. Vast sums of money were required. Investors were attracted from all over. Many English people invested. Then the English Parliament ruled that the Scheme was unlawful. The Spanish got upset. The East India Company got cross. English Investors were told to withdraw their money from the scheme. English Ambassadors in foreign lands were told to convince investors from their countries to withdraw their funds too. Scotland had to find £300000 to repay these investors. This was more than half the total cash in Scotland at the time. As a back drop to this were the debates about a Union of the Crowns of England and Scotland. Scotland raised the necessary funds and in July 1698 three ships set sail from Leith with 1200 colonists aboard. Amongst them many sons of Laird's and far fewer trades men, who had knowledge and skills to provide the manual labour required to build a colony. The first wave of settlers who had gone before them had perished. They could get no help from the English North American Colonists, as they were forbidden to help or trade. The Spanish Fleet attacked them and the English Fleet watched. Nearly all the 2000 died. Scotland was all but 'broke' and many of the Lords in Scotland thought a Union with England would be the best way out of their problems. *King William* fell off his horse and died. *Mary* had died, without any children in 1694. In 1707 Mary's sister became *Queen Anne*. Anne was delicate, her half brother *James III-(England)*, the Old Pretender, was a Catholic. When Anne died the Scots could have chosen to take *James III* as King of Scotland. The English had already decided that *Anne's* successor in England would be *George, Elector of Hanover*, a Protestant. Scots would not have wanted *James III*. He was the son of the daughter of *James VI*, who had become *James I* of England, and all but abandoned Scotland to be ruled by a succession of his minions, fewer than one hundred years before. The anti unionist *Andrew Fletcher* got 'The Act of Security' Passed. This asserted the right of Scotland to choose it's own monarch. *Dalrymple/Stair* and Pro English Lords opposed the Act of course. The English declared the Act a menace to *Queen Anne*. They persuaded *Anne* not to sign it into law….Pause…. can you see the parallel, the Scottish Parliament pass a bill, supported by a huge majority to protect Scotland after Brexit, the English Government object and pushed it into the Supreme Court…..*Queen Anne* was under the control of her ministers. The English Parliament passed an Act which stated that if Scotland failed to accept the succession of *William of Hanover* the English Fleet would blockade the seas and stop Scotland trading. More over all Scots would become aliens in England…..Pause can you see the parallel here with 'Breixt means Breixt', 'do it our way and no you cannot have an Independence Referendum', says *Mrs May*…More parallels….The English gave the Scots Lords money, lots of it. *Mrs. May* bought *Arlene Foster.* The English bought votes for a union of the Crowns. *Dalrymple/Stair* was the man of the hour, flitting from estate to estate, buying the votes. On 16 January 1707 the decision was made in the Scots Parliament. *Fletcher* had done what he could but 110 votes to 68 votes cast us into a one sided, 'incorporating union'. *Dalrymple/Stair* had thrown the cash around and told stories of the huge trade deals that would make everyone in Scotland rich, as soon as the Union was up and running. He failed to tell them of Article 22 which, provided only 16 seats in the House of Lords and only 45 in the House of commons for the Scots, so never could the Scottish representatives outvote their English counter parts. *Dalrymple/Stair* went home to bed that very day and he died! Which brings us to the situation of our times. Some of you may never have heard the story written here before, but you live with the effects of it every day, for our history is with us, and it's beat is ever there, even if the melody was lost sometime ago. The story of Protestant and Catholic, Rangers and Celtic the indigestion of our past.

(The story could have gone back to John Knox but I have tried to keep it simple, I hope I have not left out any great chunk of importance, I think you can get the idea…)

Handyman

When he arrived in this remote village Theo had said to his neighbours: "Any time I can help you just ask, if I can I will." Well they were all very pleased about that for surely Theo was a remarkable new inhabitant of this small group of a dozen houses, tucked away in the hills and all but forgotten by the outside world. It was a beautiful place Theo could hardly believe he had secured a home in the mist of such beauty. Far from the hustle and bustle of lives which are led in cityscapes, here in this landscape Theo very soon felt at home. His skills were far above amateur do-it-yourself weekend efforts. Although untrained in building, carpentry, plumbing or electrics Theo had a way with all these and you would be hard pressed to tell the difference between his workmanship and the workmanship of a full time professional. So a few weeks, after Theo had landed in this place, where the mountains were snow covered until March and the hill flowed down to the Loch, Theo found many a neighbour who was keen for his help. Cupboards were fixed, sticking doors were planed, and leaking wastes beneath kitchen sinks were repaired. All were happy with their new neighbour and gifts of food, cakes, stews, loafs of bread would be offered by way of thanks. Then one fine evening as the sunset formed a hallo about the hillside that Theo could see from his living room window, Doreen came into his house. Doreen never knocked. Theo thought that it was nice that she did not feel she had too, as if his house was just an extension of hers.

"When you have a mien-iute. Not the noo. Ma spigot's leaking." Before long Theo was on his hands and knees emptying the cupboard, which was beneath Doreen's kitchen sink. A place already familiar to him has he had replaced the sink waste only a couple of weeks before. Theo cleaned out the muck and polished off the marks which clung to the white Formica. Then he lay upon his back, with his head in the cupboard. Using a torch he looked up following the copper pipes and the connections for the washing machine into the recess, small, small, recess where resided the underside of the tap. The kitchen had been installed long ago, the copper joins were soldered and there were no valves to stem the flow of the mains water pressure under the sink. "I can see the leak. I think I shall have to get you a new spigot, next time I go to town. The leak is not much, keep that bucket under there and it will catch the drips until I can fix it." The sink was old and the standard sizes had been altered, indeed maybe there was no standard size when that sink had been installed. So it took a while to find a suitable replacement. The hardware store owner blow the dust from a cardboard box and said: "My old Dad bought this, oh a good few years back, I wondered if I would ever find a buyer, but here you are." They looked through the contents of the box and decided to make some adjustments. The storeowner said: "I can do that for you here in the shop, it will save you faffing about when you get home." So the store owner soldered some tapered copper piping to the tap base. "There you are." He said. "At the end it is fifteen mils so you can fit a valve and use the flexi hose to join the pipe work." Theo said: "Thank you for that. How much do I owe you? Lets hope I can get my hand in that tiny space. Of course the person who fitted it did not think it would ever have to be shifted, I expect they thought that sink would stay until the house fell down." It really was not a tough job but Theo had a thought in the back of his mind and he joked about it with his neighbour and her brother: "Well it should not take long, but what are the odds of something else going wrong? Maybe I get the tap out of the sink and then find this new one will not fit. Suppose something goes wrong with the stopcock. When was the last time it was turned off?" "Theo's neighbour said: "Well I lived here all my married life, and Tam's been deed five year since, I dinna ken it's ever been switched off in fifty year." Theo went into the bathroom and found that the stopcock was inside a cupboard. The handle was just protruding from a small hole in the inside of the cupboard wall. It was not easy to grip. Eventually, with a pair of pliers Theo managed to get a grip but it was impossible to turn the handle. Theo was sitting on the floor; the surroundings were dark and grubby. Really speaking Theo had plenty of other things he would have been happy to be getting on with. However he knew being a good neighbour would be good policy, he got on his feet and went to his garden shed for some WD40. He sprayed the WD40 on to the stopcock and left it for a few minutes. He gripped the stopcock handle with the pliers, the movement was easy and suddenly the handle of the stopcock came right off.

Water gushed from the mains inlet pipe and the pressure of the gush knocked the stopcock handle away from the pliers and it dropped into the hole where it had protruded moments before. There was no way to get his hand into the hole and the water was gushing and flooding the bath room: "Help, help, help." Theo shouted but the help that came was simply of no use. His neighbour and her brother could do nothing. Theo cleared the cupboard under the bathroom sink, and a glass full of false teeth fell to the floor. Theo grabbed a hammer and smashed at the inside of the cupboard. The Formica covering splintered and the chipboard beneath crumbled and the chips joined the flood of water still splashing from the pipe. Theo reached into the enlarged hole, his hand snagged on a razor sharp edge of Formica and there was blood to join the flow from the back of his hand. He could not find the handle of the tap; the hole was not large enough: "Where is the outside stop cock?" Theo shouted to his neighbour: "On the road out there." Theo went through the door and almost out into the street thinking his neighbour was right behind him, he turned and found he was alone. He turned and went back to the house, he opened the door, he shouted: "I need your help, I need you to show me where it is. We have to stop the water. The whole house will be flooded." When they found the stop cock in the road it was bunged up with soil and of course there was not a key for it. Theo went back into the bathroom and to his relief found that the water was not flooding the house but disappearing beneath the floor boards. He got a screw driver and prised a lose, short bit of floor board up. He shone a torch into the gapping caesium and realised that there was vast capacity beneath him and whatever kept the house upright was obviously porous. It was just then the Doreen's son in law arrived, a young man who was a plumber to trade. He had thinner hands and wrists than Theo and managed to get his hand in to the small gap he found the stop cock handle and pushed it back against the pressure of the flow of gushing water and managed to close the hole. Theo was in shock, a simple changing of a spigot an hour at tops and here he was drenched in cold water feeling the chill and blood dripping from his cut hand. He wrapped a clean tea towel about it and drove away to the hospital over an hour away. They gave him a Tetanus booster and sewed up the wound and he sat for a while with a sweet cup of hot chocolate. It was blowing hoolie when he got back to is wee place he let himself in and went to his bed. The sun shining through a gap in his curtains woke him next morning. Post traumatic stress had a grip and he wondered over to Doreen's house to check what had happened was not just a nightmare, then he looked at his poor hand and knew that it was all for real.

Goldfish

Iona married and after a couple of years when he still had not settled she made the bold decision to grant him his wish. They packed their meagre possessions into a hired van and drove away. Away from all she had known and all he had put up with. Later she remarked that for her it was something like pulling a cork from a bottle of wine. She was the cork and he was the corkscrew. She wished that she had not said it as soon as the words vaporised from her lips the company of lads and lassies let out a collective laugh and she turned a brighter shade of puce.

Far now from the midges and lukewarm spring sunshine she did enjoy the advantages of this new foreign world into which she had dropped. She splashed about in the shallows for although she had attended language lessons and she had experienced much pillow talk most of the words and phrases seemed to swill down the sink as water through a colander. It is like living in the gloaming she thought to herself. 'I am excited by all that is new, I do love him but everything is so, so different from the little island of my birth.'

City life was so hectic and so hot. She walked in her mind down the sandy cool beach of her 'real home' every day. Holding on to it less it evaporate into the midday sun of her new home. Her birth place had a hold of her, now she was far away from it, it kept calling her as she lay in the heat of the night and she longed for the breeze on the shore and the nip of a midge.

PB

She could do nothing she loved this man and he loved his home, to her this foreign land. He hated her Scottish world for him it was parochial and extraordinarily boring. He had fallen in love with her and no one could say he had not tried, two cold summers he had endured for this woman, listening to the Banffshire's moan about how warm the weather was as he slipped on a jumper in the middle of July. No enough was enough. He was a city man, sharp suit and haircut.

Oh how the city bored Iona, people rushing to this and that, so 'la di da', she said to herself. It was the loneliness which was the worse thing. Some days she felt like she was in a prison cell. She tried making friends, she went to the gym, she invited several different women over for coffee at the apartment. It was all very nice but the 'software' which allows communication was not installed. These people had no idea of the world from which she had come and the lack of language, friends and an understanding of the mentality of her hosts, made her feel as if she were a lonely Albatross searching for food over an endless grey and foaming South Atlantic Ocean.

So she lived her days trying to get a foot hold on this new planet, wandering the shopping centres, going to the gym. At one stage she wondered about joining a church but she was not quiet that desperate, as yet. She lived her days longing for the evening when his gorgeous face would burst through the door and brighten her darkness. Yes she did get more to grips with the language, the evening she really felt she was making some progress as soon as Alessandro arrived home, he was not through the door when she blurted out a story she thought she had understood...Her neighbour had parked her car and she had purchased a parking ticket from the machine. A rough looking man came running from the supermarket pursued by the security guard. She stuck out her leg, tripped him up and sat on him. She reached for her mobile phone and called for the police. They arrived quickly and the man was handcuffed and arrested... She told Alessandro that he had to quickly knock on the neighbour's door and check if she ad got the story right. He said: 'well done you did.' Instead of feeling elated she felt patronised, she had been so elated only moments before, now his compliment came to her like a scolding from a teacher back at home in Portknockie when she let slip a Doric word in class. It was the tone with which Alessandro said it.

When she asked could they go for a holiday, back to Scotland, he said when they had saved enough money. He told her the journey is long and expensive.

Iona had lived in his land for three years now. A year more than Alessandro had lived in hers. She could taste a resentment in the back of her mouth, it was metallic. No matter how hard she brushed her teeth it was there every day now.

PB

She studied his language, 'mama mia' and she felt she had a grasp of it. Boldly she responded to an advertisement, 'Pulitore Richiesto'-- 'Cleaner Required'. The rebuff she got was unexpected. The gruff voice said to her something along the lines of, 'if you cannot speak properly how on earth will you understand what you are required to do? Foreigners!' When Alessandro came in and she told him, he said 'oh that is nothing, probably that Scottish accent of yours. Drop that and you will have a much better chance.'

The flippancy of Alessandro's reply made Iona feel angry. He stood there and that bonnie face of his was less bonnie that it had ever been. She saw another side of him. She had given up so much to come here with him. Yes she knew it was her free choice but just what had she in return? A small, cramped apartment that had to be dusted everyday, the traffic polluted the city sent wave after wave of it into every crevasse. It was always hot, the windows were always open, the noise drove her mad. They had no air conditioning and Alessandro earned barely enough to keep them both alive. He seemed to be so pleased with himself, he was the man going out to work and supporting his wife.

She tried again and again to find a job. She tried again and again to catch some friends, in the beginning it was trying to find some friends; she had never experienced xenophobia in Portknockie, of course she was Scottish but she was sure that Alessandro had been made absolutely welcome for the two years he was there. Iona thought with the exception of a few rye comments about the English, of course we from the North

East are very welcoming—of course she had seen the Saltairs stuick in various places by a group called the 'Settler Watch', they were against English people buying up places. Here fear of strangers was her everyday experience, it was front and centre of her daily routine. Even his friends would joke about her pronunciation, she would string an hundred words together, in a somewhat reasonable fashion, maybe some of the words were a bit out of order but she tried so hard, her reward would be gales of embarrassing laugher for one word had a slightly wrong emphasis as she spat it into the air and so the meaning of the word had suddenly turned a shade of blue and there was some sexual connotation of which she had been completely unaware and which she had neither intended or even knew about. If the truth were known if they had just listened to what she was trying to say, rather than listening out for her mistakes, they would have understood perfectly well what she was trying to tell them.

Eventually she realised that if she spoke at first with a heavy Glaswegian accent in English and added a few words of Doric and they did not understand her, she could then start speaking their language, so however many mistakes, or faux pas, she had the upper hand as she was doing them a favour. She found it tiresome, no matter what she did for them, however nice she was, Iona felt as if she was in a goldfish bowl, she could see them they could see her but she could not reach out and touch them and they were not willing to touch her.

The years drifted on, in which direction she could not tell, five years in and she could hardly remember who she was. On occasion she could still hear the waves on her shore. She felt reinvented as a woman who was not meant to belong.

The children he wanted had not appeared, they could not afford the medical help that it would have taken to find out why. She felt barren and he felt that unless he passed his seed into fertile soil he would never give his mother the grand children she was demanding.

That was the most persistent and succinct of all the pressures, Iona's mother in law. The constant questions and comments about grand children and how she longed for them. Iona looked at the man she had married seven years before. In the light of her current situation he was certainly not exotic as he had been on the day of their wedding. Her best friend Ellie had warned her, Ellie had said to Iona: "You might regret marrying a foreigner. They look all right and they are exotic, for they come from far away. They come with ideas and ways which are different from our own but in the long term will those excitements last? Will they sustain a relationship and a marriage of years, and years, and weans?"

All that was haunting her when she turned a corner, on a street not far from the apartment one afternoon and walked straight into her husband Alessandro, in his suit and sunglasses, carrying his jacket on his finger, through the hanging loop, over his right shoulder. His left hand was holding the hand of a pretty, young woman, who looked half the age of Iona!

Eight years now, Iona felt like red rust dust on the floor of the garage of an old car. Her husband had no money so divorce would give her nothing to begin a new life. She limped about like a soldier who had been shot through the leg in some cruel war. Should she fight for him? No, what was the point?

She had never been apart of this place, this life she had been fooling about with all these years. The un-air-conditioned, dirty air of her apartment, the snide rebukes for, slightly mis-pronunciations, the xenophobia she felt she was surrounded by.

She wrote a card and put it in the window of the shop opposite the apartment. It was a request for a car share journey home to Scotland. She found that there was a woman who was driving north to Calais and she would travel by ferry to Dover. So a least that would be a long way of the way back home to Scotland, her home.

She packed the few things she owned in a bag, she took the months house keeping money and walked out of the door of the apartment she had loathed for so long.

The journey north was pleasant, the woman drove well and was interesting company, she had a clear voice and was pleased to hear Iona's Scottish accent. As they crossed through the alps of Switzerland and felt the cool mountain air Iona took in deep breaths of air trying to expel the dust that had choked her lungs for so long.

They sped up the autobahn, they were in Germany: "Any speed you can do," said the driver: "It's ok, unless you have an accident, then any speed becomes a bankruptcy issue!" The crossed over into France by way of Strasbourg. Then back into Germany at Saarbrucken, Schengen, Luxemborg, Belgium and France.

The driver went all the way to London, she refused to take money for fuel, the ferry trip bought no expense either for the ticket included two travellers. They drove to Kings Cross station, it was very large and very noisy. Iona had enough money to buy a train ticket home to Scotland.

Iona had heard that journey times from London to Edinburgh were improved by privatised railway companies and that fares were lower. Her journey took eight hours and sixteen minutes, the train was fifteen minutes late arriving at Waverley Station. Admittedly there was a wait for the connection train in Doncaster but Iona thought that the train had not vastly improved since she was a wee quine when her pappa had taken her to London.

Iona alighted in Edinburgh, so long she had not been there but she knew if she walked up the back from Waverley Station there was a stair-case up to the Royal Mile, if she went up there and turned right past the old Tron church and then walked up South Bridge Street before long she would arrive at her cousins house. She knew that Rachel would be surprised to see her, if she still lived there.

Iona felt a new feeling, she realised that at that moment she and she alone was the only person who knew where she was. She felt free, an escapee balloon, helium filled and gone. She dallied a little on the Royal Mile and she stopped in the Royal Oak in Infirmary Street and listened to some folk music singers, she even bought a drink, such an extravagance. She passed by some rough sleepers; she had seen none in the sun of where she came from, how did these people deal with the rain and the winter. 'What has become of the people here?' She asked herself. She noticed that things were not as clean, but this was Auld Reekie, was she ever clean? Maybe there were always rough sleepers. Well she had not been here for so long and she did not come here that often before she went to sunny climes.

Rachel did still live there, and indeed she was absolutely shocked to see Iona, after so long. 'Far hiv ye bin? Well nay bodie knew how to contact ya. How many years has it been? You did na even sent a letter! We thought something terrible had happened.' Iona was mortified. 'No, oh I am so sorry, Alessandro never had a cent to spare, he gave me exactly the money for the food and told me exactly what to buy. I had no money of my own, ever. I used to find free things, I even found a free gym.' 'How did you get here?' Iona explained and then said 'I took the months house keeping so I have a little bit of money left after buying the train ticket. Wow that was expensive! Can you help me Rachel? I am sure I have not enough money to get home.' Rachel assured Iona that she would help and she would make some phone calls around the family. 'You go and have a bath, you must be tired and I bet you are feeling mawkit (dirty). Hing ya clarty claes ower they chairs (hang your dirty clothes over the chair), you quine are aafa orra!' (you girl are very shabby)

Iona was home now it was all as she had left it but then it was all-different from when she had left it. The Doric had softened and it was less readily heard. A young woman asked Iona if she was all right. Iona said oh just waabit (exhausted), the young woman looked confused and walked away. Everything was a wee bittie thrawn (a little bit twisted). Her family were glad to find her safe and well and so glad she was back.

Ellie had married a boy fae (from) Buckie, she said. 'It was a scandal, when I told Granda I was marrying a loon (boy) fea Buckie, ya should ha seen his face it fair dirled! (vibrated) I'm glad ya back Iona. I missed ya's'

Iona was the fish out of water for a long time, but at least she could walk along by the sea again. Soon it would be the boat festival. She bought a buttery, and a baked-bean-pie and a yumyum. She got a job in MacDuff at the shell fish factory but she was leesome lane (all alone), yes quiet alone.

Not for a minute did she regret leaving the sun, the dust and the city. When people asked where she had been all these years and she told them, most of them said: "Oh how lovely! All that sun I bet you loved it." The first couple of times she tried to tell them what it was really like but she found that it was like pouring to much water into a bottle, the water just splashes over the floor. Iona found these people would soon revert to speaking of Portknockie, Iona realised this is what they know. Despite aviation and all the other forms of locomotion many people still do not travel far. Those who do often fly to a destination, are bussed to an hotel, where they sit by the pool soaking up the rays for an few days, they do one exciting excursion to the tourist shops in the village and then return home their ten days in the sun expired and almost forgotten as their plane lands them back home. They sigh: "Nice to be home, put the kettle on, we haven't had a decent cup of tea for a fortnight. Those foreigners are all very nice but they know nothing about tea bags."

Elastic has a limit, once stretched beyond the elastic limit it can no longer spring back to the original. Put it another way nobody can unlearn. Horizons once expanded can no longer be contracted. Iona had seen much in her years abroad, her perspective had changed, it was difficult to relate with many of her old friends and family members in the way she did before she went abroad all those years before. Experience had put her slightly out of their reach and although they tried and although she tried she found herself once more in a goldfish bowl and she could not touch them and the could not touch her.

Other books by

Cher Bonfis

WHO WAS KILLED?

Douglas gave up his life, and gave all he had to
Arwyn.
Then Arwyn became involved
with Raymond.
Raymond was a policeman.
He and Arwyn
made a plan to 'execute'
Douglas and steal
his house and all his funds.
Douglas found no justice
in the English legal system, and he came
face to face with real corruption.
So who was killed?

A fantastic read from beginning to end, I cannot wait to read Cher's next book. This book was exciting and kept me wanting to turn over the next page and I'm sure other people will think of that way too.   Maureen McGuire 'Waterstons'

I always love books that can tug me in and hold me there. Read this please and then tell me when you do, because I'm dying to talk to someone about this! Highly recommended! 5/5 ✹ instaws_nity 'Good Reads'

I started this story believing this was a typical psychological thriller. Much to my surprise I was taken on a very different journey, which albeit tragic, demonstrated brilliantly the altruistic nature of the main character Douglas. On occasion you want to throttle him when he fails to accept what is right in front of him but you can't help but feel affection for him at the same time.   Nicola 'Books In The Bath'

Absolutely loved this book brilliantly written, totally gripping, could not put it down, what a debut. Well done Cher Bonfis Robert A 'Amazon'

I have read a lot of books. Nothing I have ever read prepared me for the emotional storm of "WHO WAS KILLED?" by Cher Bonfis. Lewis 'Amazon'

It was amazing I loved this book. Loved how the author shaped the characters and made them so real over a lifetime of humanity. It is a thriller mystery of the classic order, setting the crime scene early but leaving the reader guessing and speculating to the very end. I do believe this author a fine wordsmith but more so she has a very deep ability to get to character detail and one can witness the coming apart at the seems of human relationships. Well written, thoroughly enjoyed. Highly recommended. 5/5 Richard Harris 'Good Reads'

WHAT HAPPENED TO KRISTOPHER ON THE ROSE TREE ESTATE?

The Bermondsey Board of Guardians purchased Shirley Lodge farm in 1899 and in 1904 they opened, what would become Shirley Oaks, a village for children who had no other place to live. The village consisted houses where the children could live. A school, a laundry, workshops, a farm and a swimming pool. The Guardians kept close supervision over the running of Shirley Oaks. In 1930 the London County Council took over until the London Boroughs were formed in 1965. Shirley Oaks was closed in 1983. In this location, and in other children's homes, and other institutions, many children found refuge and safety. There were many good and kind carers but unfortunately there were also many evil people who took advantage of their situation and subjected many children to horrific abuse. This book is an attempt to shine a broader light on the good and a brighter light on the evil.

Dedicated to all who, like me, spent their childhood within these institutions.

Review from Amazon

The subject matter is very dark but somehow Cher Bonfis manages to bring light and breath to a very difficult subject. In great detail the life of children and young people who fall into the care of the state is bought to life in an extraordinary narrative. Very well written the text has expanded my understanding of this subject which is all to often reduced by the news media to stories of abuse by carers. The contrast between the life of Kristopher and the other youngsters is as cold to hot and what happened to him was an absolute shock. Great read, great stories wrapped up in a mystery. First class and very unusual.

Thawing Snow

It would snow properly back then and the wind would lift it and drift it about the highlands. I had work in the Pitlochry Theatre and if I finished late in the evening and the snow was too treacherous I had a friend who stayed at Enochdhu. My favourite name for a village, if indeed you could call it that, ever. On the night of this story I not only had the snow to contend with but I also an abscess on my back opposite my navel but slightly lower down. Sitting in the car and driving was a torture. I was grateful to see the welcoming light outside William's front door, it was snowing again as I got my overnight bag from the back seat of my car. We had a wee bleather and then I had to sleep. The morning came bright, sunny and with a layer of freshly crisp snow all diamond studded with sparkles. We had some coffee and toast and I thought I had left my car keys in my bedroom. They were not there. I searched all about the house and outside to the car. The only things to do were to borrow William's car and to drive to the main dealer in Perth, who assured me on the phone that they could cut a key for me if I told them the registration number of the car. (Of course that would be no help later when I wanted to get into my house but one thing at a time). When I returned the new key failed to open the car door but I looked down at my feet and there were my keys glinting in the sunlight and surrounded by a patch of thawing snow.

Just in Case

I keep him locked up in a draw, that man who used to be me. What else could I do? I was like a spy in a television series my cover blown and all they could do was give me a new passport, name and a bunch of money in the bank. No opportunity to ever see friends, colleagues or family again. Left with no choice but to board the plane to Venezuela or spend the rest of my days in prison. Yes you are right I did keep some mementos of the glory days, a few newspaper clippings and other curios, dangerous, maybe but I was not ashamed of my past. What those people did to me was nothing less than evil and why should that eradicate what was once me? I am still not sure how they could have bought themselves to lie as they did. I have tried to understand how the memories of all the things, all the help, all the money I gave to these people to help their problems and make their lives good. None of that was worth anything. It made me wonder why I should ever do anything for anyone. I have met some good people since but I am more defensive than I once was. I do hope that I am never burgled and that robbers never find my secret stash of history and leave the papers scattered for the world to view. I bought a pad lock for that draw and I put those things inside a locked bag in that draw for extra safety. Just in case.

Cher Bonfis

The cover of this book entices people to buy it with the promise of 154 stories there are 157 stories
'under charge – over deliver'
I hope you have fun with the stories here
Best Wishes and thank you for your engagement with my offerings.
Best Wishes Cher

72683 words

ISBN: 978-1-7396723-4-8